Passionate Flames

Hidden Realms of Silver Lake
Book 5

Vella Day

A dark entity determined to destroy all goodness; one woman and her mate fated to take him down.

Angelique Carson had no idea that once she was let out of her hidden realm to protect the Guardians' children that her life would take a turn for the worse. Sure Thane Sinclair is her mate, but there is no way she intends to indulge in any kind of carnal pleasure until her main job is done—and that could take years.

Thane's sole purpose is to train the Guardians for battle. The moment he encounters the powerful and beautiful Angelique, however, his mission takes a back burner. Boy, does it. The only problem is that Angelique isn't interested. Could have fooled him. Every time he's around her, her sweet body pulses with desire—as does his.

At the moment though, Thane has bigger problems. Random people are showing up dead in his town, and only Angelique seems to know who's responsible. Only she's not saying.

What will Thane have to do to convince his mate that only by joining forces can these two defeat the realm's most terrifying enemy?

Chapter One

"YOU'RE PREGNANT?" ANGELIQUE Carson asked with as much surprise as she could pull off. Given her whole being was created in order to watch over the children of the Guardians, she'd been well aware of her friend's condition for a while. First came Chelsea McKinnon, who would bear a child in about six months, and now Kaleena Sinclair.

"I just found out!"

"How far along are you?"

Kaleena placed a hand on her stomach. "Two months."

Angelique smiled. "What an exciting time for you." She waved for one of the servers in her coffee shop to come over.

Shannon rushed to their table. "What can I get you?"

"Can you bring us two coffees?" Angelique asked. "We need to celebrate."

"Absolutely," her second in command said with a smile.

Not only did she want to celebrate, Angelique also wanted to spend a bit more time with her best friend. Kaleena was always working and never took enough time for herself. Now more than ever, she needed to learn to relax.

"Make mine an herbal tea," Kaleena said. Shannon nodded and hurried off. "Finn keeps telling me all of his Earth stories about how bad caffeine is for the baby."

Angelique smiled. From what she'd been told, that wasn't the case on Tarradon, but she didn't feel it was her place to say anything. "I'm surprised you left work in the middle of the day, but I'm glad you stopped by. I've missed our chats." Kaleena never played hooky.

She sighed. "Normally, I wouldn't have left, but Finn made me promise to ask if you would put a protective sac around our baby—like the one you did for Chelsea. Even though I won't be entering into any dragon battles any time soon, Finn and many of my family members are worried that something might come up where I'll be forced to fight. He wants our child to be safe."

So did she. "I totally understand."

Kaleena leaned forward. "I'll admit it bugs me they think just because I'm pregnant that I'm helpless. I'm not. I can defend myself. I've proved that time and time again. I so want to fly and engage in a little sparring." She glanced at the ceiling. "Doing battle invigorates me."

Angelique loved her friend's passion but not her decision to act recklessly, especially now. "I can teach you some meditation that will keep the baby safe once I put the protective spell on your child. I can also guide you on how to fight safely should the need arise."

Kaleena reached across the table and grasped Angelique's hand. "Really? But you're not a shifter."

"I'm not, but I've been watching fights for a while now." She winked.

Kaleena's shoulders relaxed. "You're the best. When can we get together? I can train whenever you are free."

"How about tomorrow around five? Melissa and Shannon can run the coffee shop without me for a few hours."

"Fantastic."

They discussed where to meet and decided the Sinclair Mines would provide a place where Angelique could work in private to keep the baby safe as well as show Kaleena some safe flying techniques in the large field behind the main offices.

They chatted a bit about how things were going with Angelique's new coffee shop and what else she was up to. "Things have been great," Angelique said. "Life has been calm since the incident with Chelsea. That was the last real adrenaline rush I've had. Ever since then it's been business as usual."

"That was an adventure—or rather a painful misadventure. I can't tell you how much better I feel knowing that bitch Sanditra is dead. She nearly ruined my life."

Angelique held up a finger. "As horrible as your incarceration in the castle prison was, if it hadn't been for that dark lighter, Finn might not have traveled from Earth to Tarradon to save you, which means you still might not be with your mate."

Kaleena chuckled. "There is that."

Their second round of drinks arrived, and they chatted about Kaleena's family for a bit. Angelique noticed that her friend brought up her brother Thane's name a lot. Yes, whimsical Fate had decided now that Angelique was in this human form, she should have a mate, and that mate was Thane, but it was hard not to let on that she knew.

There was no denying that the man was gorgeous, powerful, and highly driven, but Angelique's main job on Tarradon was to protect the progeny of Guardians—not have hot sex all day long. When all of the Sinclair and Caspian children were grown, she'd focus on her own pleasure.

Shattering dishes broke their intimate conversation. Angelique huffed. "Really? I guess I should deal with that. Drinks are on the house," she said as she scooted out of the booth. "Remember, tomorrow be at the mine by five."

Kaleena smiled. "I won't forget. And thank you."

Angelique went about her business, while Kaleena finished her drink before leaving. Even though running the coffee shop gave Angelique something to do while she waited for Chelsea's and now Kaleena's baby to arrive, she loved this place. It gave her a chance to talk to people all day long, which was something she sorely missed when she was a white light entity in another realm.

THE DELIVERY OF the wood Thane Sinclair had ordered for the

obstacle course he was building behind the mine was delayed until tomorrow morning. This setback put a further kink in his plans. He had already postponed all training with the Guardians, or anyone else for that matter, in order to complete the course. He needed this last piece to be finished before he could return to his fitness center in town.

Since he had some free time, he stopped by his family's mining office to see if anyone could use his help. They often asked him to run down delinquent accounts because after one look at his muscular body, the mining businessmen usually paid up pronto. He never had to threaten anyone with violence—not that he would—because the Sinclair name and his apparent fierce look were enough to squeeze the last dollar out of a person.

Thane entered the office and looked around to see who was there. His brother Declan's office was empty, but Finn McKinnon was there. He knocked on his door and entered.

"Hey," Finn said. "How's the obstacle course coming? You finish it yet?"

Thane explained about the delay. "Because of that, I have some time and wondered if you needed a hand."

Finn's brows rose. "As a matter of fact, I was just about to call you."

He hadn't expected that. "About what?"

"I have some good news."

Thane could use some of that. He pulled up a chair and faced Finn's desk. "What is it?"

"I am going to be a dad. We just found out that Kaleena is two months pregnant!"

Thane reached out and fist-pumped Finn. "Awesome, man. That's so exciting. Uncle Thane has a nice ring to it." Actually, Kaleena told him two days ago but made him promise not to let on that he knew.

"It is, but the bad news is that my stubborn mate refuses to slow down. She sees no reason not to engage in battle should the

Guardians need her."

Thane almost chuckled. "My sister always was stubborn. When she comes for her usual training, I'll make sure to take it easy."

Finn shook his head. "You know that no matter what you say, she'll work twice as hard as before to prove to you that she will always be ready—baby or not. I thought maybe you could do a one-on-one training."

What Finn said was true. Thane leaned back in his chair. "I can do that."

"I know she's free tomorrow afternoon. I can ask her to stop by here tomorrow if that works for you."

"That works. Not having anyone to compete against might keep my sister in check. I'll also do some research on how she can protect her child while she executes the maneuvers. You know as well as I that neither Declan nor Dad would ever put her in the field now."

Finn blew out a breath. "Neither will I, but sometimes she doesn't listen to anyone. Can you text her with a time and place? I want her to think it's your idea. She'll think I'm just an over protective mate if I deliver the message."

Thane smiled. "Can do."

He couldn't be more pleased that his sister was having a baby. That would make two new little Sinclair Guardians ready to greet the world. A twang of jealousy surfaced at that thought. He'd always wanted a child, but considering how Angelique always ended their far and few between dates with a chaste kiss, he wouldn't be mating with her anytime soon.

To avoid what little relationship they had between them, he'd stopped being around her. He just couldn't handle it even though his dragon kept breathing fire inside his gut from wanting her so much. After he'd fought Sanditra, Angelique had brought him back from the brink of death. From that moment on, his need for her had grown to the point of distraction.

Thane pushed back his chair. "Later, Finn."

Thane left the office and headed home. After doing a bit of

research on how to protect a pregnant dragon during battle, Thane contacted Kaleena and told her Finn had let the cat out of the bag.

"I want to go over some fighting techniques that will keep you and the baby safe."

"Thank you, but everyone is way over protective. It's not like I'm the first dragon to have a child."

He almost smiled at her defiance. "True. Can you meet me at the Sinclair Mine tomorrow at five? I want to have a one-to-one with you. Onlookers tend to distract."

She hesitated for a moment and then practically giggled. "That's perfect timing!"

In all honesty, Thane thought Kaleena would balk at having to tone down her training. He was just pleased he'd dodged an argument.

Assuming the wood he needed would be delivered tomorrow morning as promised, he would be at the mines all day working on the final stages of building the obstacle course. Having her come to the mines around five would be ideal.

In need of some relaxation after the mess up with the material delivery, Thane headed over to Wing's Bar. He loved they had a flat roof on which to land, along with a stairwell that exited out to the back of the bar. Not that all of the customers were dragon shifters, but the majority were. Since parking around the bar was a bitch, flying was much easier.

Tonight was Finn's night off to bartend, so Thane ordered his scotch from Barry who unfortunately wasn't as generous with the whisky as Finn. Once Barry delivered his drink, Thane spun around on his bar stool to watch the patrons. People watching was one of his favorite pastimes.

Halfway into his drink, his skin prickled, and his gold scales flickered under his skin. Shit.

She's here! his dragon announced with too much glee.

And here I thought I'd have a nice relaxing evening.

Now's your chance to ask her out.

Angelique messes with my libido too much, so cool it.

His dragon huffed but thankfully kept quiet. While Thane always enjoyed watching his beautiful mate, when she acted as if he wasn't anything special, it drove him crazy. She might only be a white lighter and not a shifter, but she'd even admitted one night that they were mates. Why she wouldn't do anything about it was anyone's guess. Hell, he could see from the way her eyes sparkled and her skin pulsed white that she wanted him. Something was holding her back, only she refused to tell him what it was. But Thane Sinclair wasn't a Guardian for nothing. He'd find out one way or the other.

Laughter floated his way. When he spotted his fair-haired beauty, his pulse soared once more. Thane waited for Angelique to turn toward him and at least wave, but instead she wove her way down the aisle between the tables, smiling at two of her friends. One of the women with her was Melissa, but he couldn't remember the other one's name. Both, however, worked at her coffee shop.

He tossed back the rest of his drink. While Thane should leave, he wasn't ready. Just because the woman who made his scales glow and his cock hard had entered the bar, it didn't mean he should cut short his relaxation time.

Soon, this teasing affair had to end though. Angelique was his mate, and he was determined to win her over.

"THANE'S STARING AT you again," Melissa said with too much glee.

"Is that so?" Angelique said, attempting to act nonchalant. She never should have sat in the booth facing him, but she couldn't help it. Thane was hot, especially with his tanned skin, short dark hair, and square jaw—not to mention those piercing green eyes.

Angelique probably should give some excuse why she had to leave, but she'd asked her two employees out for a drink to celebrate the half-year anniversary of the opening of Angelique's Coffee Shop, and she'd be damned if Thane Sinclair was going to ruin it.

"Hey, if you don't want him, would you mind if I give him a shot?" Melissa asked.

An unexpected and unwanted surge of lust slammed into her that she refused to call jealousy. Sure, they were mates, but Fate never said she needed to do anything about it right away. Angelique would have urged Melissa to have a go at him, but her friend would only be disappointed when she found out nothing could come from it. Thane seemed to have his sights on Angelique, and she suspected no other woman would be able to change his mind. "I heard he's engaged or something."

Melissa's eyes widened. "Really? You'd never know it. I've never seen him with anyone. Remember, when he used to come into the coffee shop when we first opened?"

How could she not? Her white light had pulsed from the inside out. "I recall him coming in a few times."

"He was always alone. If he has a lady friend, where is she?"

"Next time we chat, I'll ask him." Angelique smiled, despite the lie that just came out of her mouth. As if some guardian angel was watching, a server rushed over to take their drink orders.

Angelique looked at her two friends. "How about we split a pitcher of Sangria?"

Before Finn arrived from Earth, the drink didn't exist. He'd introduced Edendale to the delicious concoction, and it was a big hit at the bar.

"I'm game," Shannon said.

"Me too," Melissa chimed in.

Their server told them he'd be right back with their drinks.

Angelique had been looking forward to tonight, but maybe it had been a mistake to come to the one place Thane often frequented. After Kaleena had talked about how Thane had been building some huge obstacle course, her imagination had gone wild thinking about what his calloused palms could do to her body. She hated when she let her imagination run wild, but somehow she was powerless to stop herself from thinking about him. Had she known he'd be there tonight, she might have suggested a different location.

Or…had she secretly wanted to run into him? Sheesh. She was slowly falling apart with indecision, which wasn't good on any level. At some point, she just might have to jump his bones to get him out of her system. Fate had been cruel in giving her two tasks: ensure the safety of the Guardian children and deal with a mate. One or the other she could handle. Both at the same time were just too much.

"Why don't you go over there and talk to him?" Shannon urged. "I swear I saw his arms pulse gold when he looked at you. He wants you." She sighed. "I bet he is as beautiful a dragon as he is a man."

Angelique never should have told these humans that Thane was a shifter, but when they'd asked for details about how she had helped save Chelsea from the dark lighter, she had to give them some information.

"Thane Sinclair is a warrior. He spends his whole life training people to fight. He's just not my type." She hoped no darkness started to grow inside her from that lie.

In truth, growing up, Angelique never believed it was possible for her to have a mate given she was pure light, but once she saw Thane, she understood why Fate had paired him with her. Her purpose in life had always been to help people from afar. It wasn't until she was called to this realm that she'd even had a body. Too bad, it had to be one that was sensitive to a man's touch—or rather to Thane's touch.

When Angelique had first shown up in Thedia province, it had taken her months to interact with people effectively. She had to learn who was good and who was bad, but when she'd helped the deserving ones, it had been a rush.

To fully understand what humans and shifters were thinking and how and why they reacted the way they did, she'd engaged in many activities—the most pleasurable of which was sex. Even though it was nice, she was a bit disappointed that the world didn't stand still as so many had claimed it would—that was until she went near Thane. No, they'd not engaged in *that* carnal pleasure—and wouldn't for a long time—but the few kisses she'd gotten when he said goodnight had done more to stimulate her than any full-blown encounter she'd ever had.

She almost smiled at the memory of how her body had screamed *mate-mate* as soon as she met him. Finding Thane so soon after her arrival to this realm had been a shock, but there was nothing wrong with waiting a few hundred more years—assuming she could hold out that long.

Chapter Two

NOT WANTING KALEENA to wait for her, Angelique arrived at the Sinclair Mines a few minutes early. She shouldn't have been surprised to find Thane standing outside the office, but she was. She thought he'd be busy building something or training a group of dragon shifters—not just waiting around in front of the office doing nothing. While she wasn't pleased that she'd have to tamp down her urges, she would have some satisfaction when Kaleena told him that she'd picked Angelique to be the one to protect her precious child.

Angelique cut the engine to her car and slipped out. Thane turned and lasered her with a stare. His brows were pinched more than usual as he strode toward her. What was up with that aggressive behavior?

"What are you doing here?" he asked. His tone came out even and not accusatory, but his tight jaw implied he wasn't happy she'd invaded his territory. Good. That made keeping her distance easier.

Angelique stood up straighter. She had to assume that Kaleena had told her family that she was pregnant. "Kaleena stopped by the coffee shop yesterday and asked if I would create a protective sac for her unborn child."

His brows rose. "Is that so? Then why is she meeting me here at five to learn how to fight while pregnant?"

Shit. "She has no intention of fighting. In case she is ambushed or something, she asked *me* to give her some pointers."

He laughed. "You? How can a mere white lighter teach someone to do battle? You can't even fly."

"Not by myself, but I understand the dynamics of the event

rather well. Perhaps your memory is faulty, but during Declan's and your recent battle against the dark lighter Sanditra, I was the one who saved the day."

"He told me, but I think my brother was hallucinating at the time."

Angelique debated whether to give him the details about how she had inhabited Declan's body and healed him from the inside out while he was in flight, but then a whoosh of air sounded behind her followed by the flapping of wings. Angelique spun around to see Kaleena land and transform. As much as she wanted to tell this pig-headed man that he was wrong about what really happened during the encounter, now wasn't the time.

"Hey, sis," Thane said, as he kissed her cheek. He looked over at Angelique. "Let's see what she has to say about her request for help," Thane said acting way too smug.

Angelique rushed toward her friend and hugged her. "Why did you ask Thane here?" she whispered.

"Thane said he wanted to tailor the training to my pregnancy. I figured the more help the better."

Angelique couldn't argue with that, but did Kaleena have to ask both of them here at the same time? It didn't matter. Angelique would deal. "Fine. Let's go inside where I can put the protective spell on your baby before you take to the sky."

"Sure." Kaleena turned to Thane. "I'll be right out. Where will you be?"

"In the field out back."

Angelique didn't miss the slight lowering of his lids. Competitive bugger.

Together, she and Kaleena went inside to one of the spare rooms at the safe house. For some reason, Angelique felt as if she was being set up, but she didn't want to upset her friend by accusing her of doing something so underhanded. Most likely, Thane had told his sister that he and Angelique were mates but what happened between them wasn't anyone's business.

Once they reached the room where Kaleena stayed when she was in need of protection, they stepped inside. She spun toward Angelique. "I hope you're not mad that I asked both of you to meet at the same time. I just figured it would be best if you and Thane were on the same page."

That wasn't going to happen anytime soon, but she was a grown woman who could keep her emotions in check. "Sure. No problem."

As soon as Kaleena stretched out on the bed, Angelique placed her hands on Kaleena's abdomen and felt her life force loud and clear. A smile crossed her lips. To think this child would help guide the Guardians someday.

Closing her eyes, Angelique said her protective chant as she sent her white light inside Kaleena. Because Kaleena was a white lighter herself, it took far less power to encase the child in the sac than it had when she'd performed this spell with Chelsea. Now nothing would happen to the baby.

"Ready to take to the skies?" Angelique asked once she was done.

"Absolutely."

They walked outside and around to the back. Angelique halted, stunned at the intricate and massive obstacle course before her. "Wow. This is how you train?" she asked, highly impressed.

The first obstacle involved climbing up a twenty-foot tall, sloped wall that dropped down the other side onto a sandpit. From there it required the person to step between tires before swinging from one overhead hook to another using a ring to hold onto. The expansive course seemed to test endurance, agility, coordination, and strength. "I hope you don't plan to run this," Angelique said to Kaleena.

"I don't—at least not anytime soon. I'm really just interested in learning some maneuvers should I be attacked."

"Do attacks happen often?" Angelique asked. She didn't want to give away just how much she knew about the Guardians.

"No, but they can happen at any time."

Thane strutted over. "Ready for your training?" he asked Kaleena, not even glancing at Angelique.

She couldn't help but intervene. "I hope you aren't going to ask Kaleena to run this course. It's not safe for someone in her condition."

He moved closer to her, the air around her evaporating. "This simple course? Kaleena could do it no problem, but since she's not in training, I see no reason for her to bother."

"I agree. The twenty-foot drop on the other side of that first wall wouldn't be good for her child."

"Kaleena could handle it. We Sinclairs are tough."

From his tone, he was kidding—or was he? Angelique couldn't help but take his comment as a challenge. "Are you implying I'm not tough enough to handle this *simple* course?" Angelique had no idea if she could make it through or not.

Of course, if she used any of her magic, she could beat him in a heartbeat.

"I'm not implying anything, but if you'd like to race me some time, I'd be happy to beat you."

A thousand responses flew to her tongue, but before she could say anything, Kaleena cleared her throat. "Ah, I think we are here to help me," Kaleena said, almost laughing.

Angelique stepped back and held up her hands. "By all means. I'd love to see what Thane thinks are safe fighting techniques."

"I'll be happy to show you how it's done. Too bad you aren't a dragon. Otherwise, I could help train you too."

She definitely didn't need any of his help, but she didn't want to get into an argument in front of Kaleena.

Wanting to give these two plenty of room, Angelique moved back to the edge of the field. If Thane put Kaleena's health in jeopardy, she'd step in. While she was about fifty feet away, she was still close enough to hear his instruction. Thane listed which maneuvers Kaleena needed to avoid since they would be dangerous. The most important thing for her was not to expose her stomach to her attacker. While being on her back was often the most efficient way to reach the other dragon's heart, a quick swipe to her gut could do irreparable damage. Angelique had to admit his advice was sound.

When the two of them shifted, their beauty nearly took her breath away. Yes, she had witnessed Thane fight Sanditra, the dark witch who had tried to turn Kaleena from a white lighter into a dark lighter, but now that his life wasn't in peril, Angelique could admire his shiny black scales interspersed with gold ones. No one was more regal than Thane Sinclair.

She was so entranced with the fluidity of their flight that she was caught off guard when a wave of darkness reached her from behind. She whipped around to see a tall, handsome man approach.

If he worked at the mines, she needed to warn Thane that he might be up to no good.

"They're beautiful, aren't they?" he asked, nodding to the dragons, not bothering to look at her.

Not wanting to give away that she was aware of his dark aura, she kept her response simple. "Yes."

He finally faced her, smiled, and then held out his hand. "I'm Denalt."

She loathed to touch his hand, but she didn't want to let him know that she knew he was evil personified. "I'm Angelique. Do you work here?" That sounded nicer than *get the fuck away from here*.

"I delivered some wood for the obstacle course for Thane this morning. I just wanted to make sure it was enough."

That was a bit anticlimactic, though he wouldn't announce he was there to put some kind of spell on someone. The man gave off a slightly different vibe than Sanditra, implying he might be even darker. "He shouldn't be too much longer," she said.

Angelique wanted the training session to end soon because being with this man gave her the willies. She might have left had Denalt not been watching Kaleena so intently. So much darkness radiated out of him, it made her wonder why Thane ever dealt with him in the first place. Most likely, he couldn't sense this dark lighter's aura very well.

Thane must have figured something was up, because he shot to the ground, shifted, and came over to them. Kaleena landed right behind him.

Angelique waved to her friend. "Kaleena. Come back to the office for a second. I forgot to do something." She held her gaze, hoping her friend would take the hint.

"Sure."

The two of them left, leaving Thane to deal with Denalt. As soon as the waves of darkness diminished, Angelique relaxed.

"What did you forget to do?" Kaleena said a little out of breath.

"I lied. I wanted to get us away from that man. He was giving me the creeps."

"I didn't feel anything. Then again, I was still high from engaging in the mock battle. I wasn't focusing on him. Who was he?" Kaleena asked.

"Some guy who delivered wood to Thane this morning. He was following up on the order—or so he said. He seemed rather dark to me." She didn't want to scare Kaleena, so she kept her real thoughts to herself.

"I hadn't noticed, but I think I've seen him before in town."

"Just in case, I'd steer clear of him." Angelique nodded to Kaleena's stomach. "How's the baby?"

Kaleena placed her hands on her belly and then smiled. "All is well. I think flying excites her—or him."

"That's awesome."

Kaleena squeezed Angelique's arm. "Thanks again for helping me."

"Anytime."

Kaleena looked down at her hands. "I need to tell you something."

Angelique wasn't sure she liked the sound of that. "Was is it?"

"I know I said I wanted to train so I could fight during pregnancy, but that was a ruse to get you and Thane together."

Angelique placed a hand on Kaleena's arm, not sure how she felt about that. "I appreciate that, but trust me, I don't need any help."

"You two would be perfect for each other. I can see it in Thane's eyes that he wants you."

She inhaled. "Did he tell you we were mates?"

"He didn't have to. I could tell, but it seems like you needed a little encouragement." She shrugged. "From the way you two interact, I can tell my plan failed."

She didn't want her well-intentioned friend to feel bad. "It's fine. Really. I just need more time. Opening the shop has consumed me."

Kaleena smiled. "I get it, but throw him a bone every once in a while."

Angelique laughed. "You mean smile at him?'

Her friend's eyes sparkled. "Yes. Exactly. It wouldn't hurt to go out to dinner with him either. He's a really nice guy and needs to focus on something other than work."

She understood. "I'll think about it. I'm just glad you don't plan on fighting."

"No way. Today was the last of it."

Kaleena hugged her goodbye, shifted, and flew back toward town. Wanting nothing more to do with Denalt and his bad vibes, Angelique hopped in her car and returned to the coffee shop. All during the drive something bothered her, but she couldn't identify exactly what it was. Kaleena was a white lighter yet she hadn't sensed the man's darkness. Did that mean Angelique had overreacted? She honestly couldn't recall that ever happening before. Because she'd come from a closed realm where both light and dark entities were released every so often, she of all people would be more sensitive to this kind of aura than most.

Whatever. Denalt hadn't acted inappropriately, and as long as the man meant no harm to Kaleena, Angelique could live with it.

BY THE NEXT morning however, Angelique still hadn't shaken this feeling of imminent danger. Most likely she was a little upset that

Thane had been the one to train Kaleena, and her uneasiness had nothing to do with Denalt. Just to be safe though, she wanted to warn Thane. He'd probably say he and Finn were perfectly capable of taking care of Kaleena, and that Denalt posed no threat. Normally, he would be right, but the more she thought about it, the more she was convinced Denalt had been taken over by a dark entity from her realm. If that were the case, he'd be way too powerful for any dragon to take down.

Around four thirty, she'd had enough of second guessing herself on how to handle things. It was time to come clean about who she was and where she came from. Melissa was in the office working on the receipts, and Shannon was overseeing the coffee shop.

Angelique tapped on the office door and entered. "Hey, I have some errands to run. I doubt I'll be long, but if I'm not back by seven, can you lock up?"

"Sure. Is everything okay?"

Angelique painted on a smile. "Yes, thank you."

Not sure if Thane would be at his studio in town or doing something at the mine, she called him instead of heading over.

"Angelique! To what do I owe this pleasure? Calling to admit I'm more than capable to train my sister?"

He didn't have to sound so surprised that she'd called. Okay, maybe she was often standoffish, but she had her reasons. "Can we talk?"

"I'm always up for seeing you."

The few times they'd gone out, when she'd leaned over and given him a peck on the cheek goodbye, he'd clearly wanted more. "Where are you?"

"At the mine. I just put the finishing touches on the obstacle course."

"I'll be there shortly."

"Why don't you stop home and grab something you can work out in."

She smiled. "Don't tell me you want to show me how hard your course is."

He laughed. "You said it looked easy. We could race. If you win, then I'll definitely have to make some alterations."

"I love challenges, but be forewarned, I plan to win." Thane had the ability to change her mood from dark to light with just a look or a cute comment.

"Oh really? If that's the case, I'll need a leg up. Why don't you wear one of your Angelique's Coffee Shop uniforms?"

She had no intention of wearing a dress while climbing a twenty-foot wall. It didn't matter they'd be next to each other. "I'll wear something a bit more suitable, thank you."

Damn. Why did she let him bait her? She better beat his ass. If he won, he'd be insufferable, and she couldn't let that happen. The question was whether she could win without resorting to magic?

Most definitely, she decided. Or maybe not.

"Let the games begin."

Chapter Three

THANE DISCONNECTED, SHOCKED yet delighted that Angelique had called. He would have been grinning ear to ear had she not sounded so worried. However, the moment he challenged her to a race, her tone had lightened.

She'd be there soon. Wanting to make sure the course was perfect, he rushed toward the twenty-foot curved wall and scrambled to the top. He was able to grasp the top with the tip of his fingers. Using his biceps, he pulled himself up as he swung his leg over the wooden top. Twisting around, he lowered himself over the other side and dropped to the sand pit below. He was halfway to the tires when his body surged with lust. Angelique was here.

She'd arrived faster than he'd anticipated. When he stepped around the wall, he halted at the vision before him.

Mate, mate, his dragon panted.

Don't I know it, but we need to stay calm and not act rashly.

You might, but I don't have to.

Thane wished his dragon would go back to sleep. Ever since Angelique had moved to Edendale, his dragon had been insufferable, but he could understand why. Angelique was gorgeous. Today, she was wearing a bright purple, body-hugging top that contrasted with her milky white skin, and the tight, black leggings accentuated her curvy ass and showed off her ridiculously long legs. He'd never seen her in anything so revealing, which made his scales pulse gold under his skin. With his tan however, the scales weren't too visible thank goodness. He didn't need her to know how much he wanted her—mate or not.

Angelique's long blonde hair was pulled back into a braid, looking like she was ready to try the course. On her feet were what looked like rock climbing shoes, which would help her climb over that first hurdle quite well. Smart.

He strode toward her, only now realizing he was a bit sweaty. "Your call sounded urgent. What's up?" Thane asked with possibly too much cheer.

"We need to talk."

He shielded his brow from the sun. The backside of the curved wall would provide some shade. "Come on over here where we can chat."

He dropped down onto the sand pit. She raised her eyebrows but then joined him. "What do you know about Denalt?" she asked.

"Denalt? You mean the guy who delivered my wood to build the course?"

"Yes."

"What about him? I've known him for years." She glanced away, almost as if this wasn't the answer she was expecting. "What's this about?"

"You know I'm a white lighter, right?"

"Seeing how you were able to scare the crap out of Sanditra before Declan killed the dark lighter, I figured it out."

She bit down on her bottom lip, and his dragon roared.

Stay down, boy, he commanded his animal.

"I did a little more than that, but that's not why I'm here. When Denalt walked up behind me, I experienced a wave of darkness— even more powerful than what radiated off Sanditra."

Thane shook his head. "You have to be wrong. Denalt is a good guy."

She held up her hands. "All I know is that I had a sense that he showed up to harm someone. He couldn't take his eyes off of Kaleena, which really worries me."

Thane stiffened. "He's not even a dragon shifter. Hell, Denalt can't shift at all." What wasn't she telling him? "Did he say something to you? If he did, I'll kick his ass."

Thane started to rise, and when she planted a hand on his arm, his dragon breathed fire, wanting more.

"No. He didn't say or do anything. I just came to warn you he could be trouble."

Thane clenched his jaw. "If it will set your mind at ease, I'll tell him not to come around here anymore. The course is finished so I don't need his services or his wood any longer. If he snoops around you, let me know. I'll make sure he doesn't bother you again."

Finally, a small smile lifted her lips. "I can take care of myself."

Wanting to put a bigger smile on her lips, he jumped up and held out his hand. "I'm sure you can, but I'd like to see just how much you can handle yourself. We have a race to run, remember? Just don't beat me too badly." He doubted she'd even finish half of the course. Much of the exercises required a lot of upper body strength. From her smooth arms, she wasn't built for power. What she was built for was... Damn. He needed to keep his mind out of the gutter.

"Can your ego handle defeat by a non-shifter?" she asked in a surprisingly flirtatious tone.

He wasn't going to lose. "Of course."

"What does the winner get?" she asked, pushing the boundaries once more.

A romp in bed with me? Like that would ever happen. He changed his tactic. "You can buy me a shot of whisky."

"And if I win?"

"I'll buy you dinner."

She shook her head. "Where's the equality in that? Loser buys dinner regardless. Plain and simple."

He held up his hands. A date it was. "Fine by me. Let me go over the course with you. Some of the exercises are not obvious about what needs to be done."

"I'm sure I can figure out what to do."

"Nope. I don't want you whining about how the race wasn't

fair." Most of the obstacles were rather simple but not all of them. "The trickiest of them is the barrel walk. This will test your speed and agility." He led her halfway across the field to where he had five barrels next to each other with a metal rod through the middle of each one, elevated four feet off the ground. The rods allowed the barrels to spin freely. Running across all five before landing onto a mat required a high degree of precision. He'd seen semi-professionals do it in the Tarradon Ninja Warrior show, but when Thane had first tried it, he'd slipped and fallen into the mud puddle below. He bet Angelique with her long legs, wouldn't reach the third barrel without sliding off. He hoped she didn't become too upset when dirt caked her nice round butt.

Thane demonstrated where to place her feet in order to make it across without slipping. "The rest is fairly obvious," he said. "For the last obstacle, grab hold of the swinging tire and pump a few times to gain momentum. Your goal is to reach the hanging netting. It's pretty loose, so hold on tight. Crawl on the underside until you reach the mat, and then run another one hundred yards. The first to reach the stone statue wins."

"Let's do this," she said with more joy than he expected.

For a brief moment, there was a hint of fear inside him. No one had ever beaten him in any course. He was sure he had nothing to worry about. Regardless of the outcome, he'd have a nice dinner with his mate.

"Race you back to the starting point," she said.

Before he could respond, Angelique took off, arriving at the towering wall before he did. Damn. Maybe he couldn't afford to go easy on her. His strategy had been to keep a little behind her, winning only at the end. After seeing her speed and agility, perhaps he'd go all out for the first half and then see how far she lagged behind before making any adjustments. Humiliating her wouldn't help his cause.

Angelique stood in front of her twenty-foot wall while he went to the identical station ten feet away.

"Don't be a sore loser," she said, taunting him.

"Not a problem. You're going down." She laughed once more, jacking up his libido. "Ready?" he asked. She nodded. "On the count of three. One. Two. Three."

Even Thane understood how important it was not to lose concentration, but he couldn't help but watch her. If she only made it halfway up the first incline, the slide back to the ground might injure her.

To his surprise, she raced up the incline as if it were flat. With incredible agility, she swung her legs over the top and dropped to the sand pit below, landing gracefully on both feet. Without taking a moment to breathe, she sprinted toward the row of tires.

Shit. Thane was a good three seconds behind. Not letting himself watch her anymore, he sped through the tires and then grabbed the metal ring eight feet above the ground, ready to swing the twenty feet in the air. Angelique had to crouch down and then jump up to reach the ring, costing her precious time.

Every time he looked over at her though, she was neck-and-neck with him, and his admiration grew. He had no idea white lighters had this much talent. Thane was convinced the barrel walk would be her undoing. To his surprise, she sprinted across the top with ease. Just before the fifth barrel, she leapt over it and dropped to the mat below. He landed a second later but managed to outrun her for the last stretch, reaching the statue less than a second before she did.

Sweat poured off his body, while Angelique merely glowed. If he hadn't seen it for himself, he would have thought she hadn't even exercised.

She faced him and held out her hand. "You won. Congrats."

As soon as he shook it, his dragon woke up, and his claws tried to extend. "You did amazingly well. I've run this course at least ten times."

She planted her hands on her hips and bent over to catch her breath. "What do you say we do it again? Double or nothing."

If the reward would be sex, he'd go ten more times. He'd even let her win. "I think you've had enough."

Angelique straightened. "Let me be the judge of that." Her tone came out a bit too defensive despite being winded.

"Okay, okay, but how about we walk back to the start?"

She smiled and then winked. "Deal."

Thane couldn't decide if he should let her win this time or not. She had almost beaten him the first time, but he figured it was beginner's luck. In the end, he decided Angelique would be pissed if she thought he didn't give his best.

Once at the start, he looked over at her. She was inhaling deeply and then exhaling slowly as if she wanted to be ready for the race of a lifetime. "Why don't you count down this time?" he said.

"I can do that. Ready?"

"Yes."

"On three. One. Two. Three."

They took off at the same time. Keeping his focus this time, he raced up the wall, swung his leg over, and dropped down, sand flying everywhere. The tire run was easy as were the next few obstacles. Angelique swore a few times, but he refused to look over at her. If she beat him, he wanted her to legitimately win—not that that would happen. After all, he'd designed the course and practiced on each obstacle many times.

When he reached the barrel run, he dashed over the first four, but his foot didn't hit dead center on the fifth one, causing the barrel to spin. Off balance, Thane had to dive toward the mat instead of leaping onto it with both feet. Hands extended, he managed to do a front flip. While he landed okay, he'd lost precious time. Hopefully, he'd make it up on the last run.

Out of the corner of his eye, he estimated Angelique to be about a second ahead of him. While he swung on the rings well and grabbed the netting at a good spot, he was so pissed at himself for having missed that fifth barrel that he faltered a bit in reaching the final pad. Despite a superfast acceleration to the statue on his part, she beat him.

She raised her arms in victory and jumped up and down. "Gotcha!"

He laughed. "You still owe me dinner."

"No way. You agreed to double or nothing."

"Damn. Okay, but you can pay for drinks."

"Deal."

He appreciated her good nature. "What time should I pick you up tonight?"

Something strange crossed her face, but then she said, "How about six?"

"Highlander's Steakhouse work for you?"

"Yes."

Thane wasn't pleased he lost to anyone, but if he had to lose, he was glad it was to Angelique. He'd always believed she was special, but this proved she was going to be a challenge in all aspects of his life.

"I'll walk you back to your car."

"Thanks."

Even though they had sprinted the course twice, Angelique almost looked dry. Him? He was downright wet. Once in front of the office building, he opened the car door for her. "See you at six then."

As soon as she left, Thane needed some time to think. He shifted and took to the skies. Yesterday had started off a little contentious since he suspected his sister had played both of them against each other. Kaleena had to have figured out that Angelique wasn't the best person to help her with fighting techniques, but he certainly couldn't put any kind of protective sac around her baby either. He and Angelique complemented each other quite well.

As he soared over town, he spotted the lumberyard where he'd purchased the wood for his course. Thane had worked with Denalt for years and had never sensed anything dark about the man, but if Angelique thought there was something evil inside the guy, it was Thane's duty to check him out.

He decided to stop over at the yard and tell Denalt he'd made some of the women uncomfortable and to ask him not to come over again. That should give Angelique some peace of mind. Only then could he focus on being with her for the evening—an evening he was sure he wouldn't forget for a long time.

Chapter Four

ANGELIQUE NEVER SHOULD have agreed to that stupid bet. Beating Thane meant she'd have to go out to dinner with him. Losing to him meant the same thing. Sheesh. Dating him right now just wasn't smart. An evil existed in town, and she needed to make sure it didn't harm anyone. Sure, she'd lived with dark entities her entire life, but this was different—this time she believed that when it had taken a human form, it was far more dangerous, because she couldn't sense it from afar.

For now though, she'd go out to dinner with Thane. She'd warned him that Denalt might cause some harm to Kaleena. It was all Angelique could do.

Or was it?

For today, yes.

After dinner, she'd give Thane a chaste kiss goodnight like she had the last few times and then keep her distance. Denalt had to be stopped, and she was the only one capable of doing that.

After a quick shower, Angelique pawed through her closet, trying to decide what to wear. Going sexy would have been the easy route, but it wasn't the signal she wanted to give off to Thane. She'd already presented herself as a jock and a businesswoman, so she should probably keep with that theme. It was definitely safer. Being near her mate caused her all sorts of issues. It was why she didn't pursue him.

The restaurant he was taking her to was fairly dressy, so faded jeans and a baggy T-shirt were out. Fancy dresses were not her thing though. In the end, she went with black slacks and a peach colored, long sleeve V-neck pullover that didn't show any cleavage. Because Thane was about six-five, she wore boots with two-inch heels. Being in the sun a lot today had given her some color, but her skin still remained pale. A slightly darker foundation would have enhanced her looks, but that wasn't something she was comfortable with. Pink lipstick and a bit of blush and eye shadow were all she was willing to do.

Angelique had just walked into the living room when someone knocked at precisely six o'clock. It was Thane. The man was prompt if nothing else.

When she pulled open the door, she stilled. She didn't need to be a white entity to know something had happened—something bad. Thane had showered and put on jeans and a white T-shirt, but he wasn't wearing anything suitable for the Highlander's Steakhouse. Crease lines furrowed his brow.

"Come in and tell me what's wrong," she said.

He strode past her and then faced her. "We need to talk."

That had been her line this afternoon. Her pulse skyrocketed at his dismay. "Okay. About what?"

"Denalt."

Her heart nearly stopped. "Did he do something?"

Thane spun to face her. "He's dead."

"What?" Angelique almost couldn't comprehend what that might mean. "How?"

He shook his head. "Mind if we call in dinner? I'm not in the mood to go out tonight. Also, it will be easier to discuss this without others listening in."

"Of course." It was time to tell him some truths anyway—or as much as she thought Thane could handle.

He pulled out his phone. "The Hillside Café is still open, and they deliver. What are you in the mood for?"

Angelique was impressed that he could ask her about food after finding out a friend had died, but perhaps they weren't that close. Even though she wasn't hungry after hearing the news, Thane seemed to be. "Anything."

"Chicken Parmesan?"

"I'm fine with that."

He called in the order and then disconnected. "Have any booze? I could use some." He marched toward the kitchen.

Clearly, Thane was more upset than he let on. "Tell me what is going on," she said following him.

He spun to face her. "I actually liked Denalt—or rather I did until you told me he was some dark soul."

That's because the man at the field wasn't really Denalt. "I have red wine. Is that okay?"

"Anything is fine."

While Angelique retrieved the bottle and glasses, her mind spun. "When did he die? We just saw him yesterday."

"I'm not sure. After you left the course this afternoon, I decided to have a discussion with Denalt about staying away from the mine. I wanted to tell him that I didn't need more wood and that he made you uncomfortable. The last thing any of us needed or wanted was to put Kaleena's life or yours in jeopardy."

His life might be at stake too. "Thank you for believing me when I said that there was something bad about him. Or should I say, something bad had happened to him."

He stilled. "What do you mean?"

"You tell me what you know about his death, and then I'll fill you in with what I think might have happened." She poured him a glass and handed it to him.

Thane tossed back a good portion of the drink. "I stopped over at the lumberyard, where they told me that Denalt hadn't shown up for work today. They said that was rare for him. After they gave me his home address, I headed over to his place."

She loved how protective he was of not only his family and her, but of his friends as well. "But he didn't answer the door," Angelique added, dread filling her.

"No. He lives in a house on the edge of town. When I looked in the window, I saw him lying on the floor. I broke in, and what I saw scared the shit out of me. Trust me, that's hard to do, because I've seen a lot."

Angelique poured herself a glass, refilled his, and then re-corked the bottle. "Let's sit in the living room. What was so horrible? Surely, you've seen a dead body before." After all, he was a Guardian. She could guess what he was going to say, and anyone would have freaked out.

"It wasn't like anything I've ever seen before."

Now was the time to fill in the gaps. "I take it he had a large hole burned in his body, almost as if fire had escaped from that spot." While she'd only seen that happen once before, she knew what had caused it.

Thane set down his drink, removed her glass from her fingers, and motioned she sit. "Holy fuck. What aren't you telling me?"

Where should she begin? "Drink up. You'll need it."

Thane dipped his chin. "Angelique?"

"Okay, okay. The man you've known as a friend had most likely been inhabited by a dark entity—though I'm not sure inhabited is the best word. Taken over might be better."

"Inhabited, taken over. Call it what you want. Can a dark lighter even do that?"

"No, a dark lighter can't." She blew out a breath. This was going to be more difficult than she thought. "It was only after you confirmed there was a burn mark that I realized my worst nightmare is coming true."

He scooted over. "Tell me what you mean. Don't skip over anything. I can handle it."

She wasn't so sure. Her stomach was doing little flips, and her heart was racing so fast, it scared even her. "I'm what you call a white entity."

"Many in my family are white lighters. That's not a big deal." He held up his hand. "I didn't mean it like it sounded."

She lowered his hand, and the skin-to-skin contact gave her the courage to continue. "This is going to sound really crazy, but I'm a bit more than just a white lighter. I come from a realm where only light and dark entities exist. We aren't born with bodies, which means we aren't your ordinary white lighter, if there is such a thing as ordinary."

He chuckled, but it was filled with disbelief. "You're telling me you aren't real? Or that you're immortal?"

"No. I'm very real. At least, now I am. I'm also mortal now." She looked at the ceiling and exhaled. "It's complicated."

"You're a bright and competent woman. Demystify it for me." Gone was any cheer. In its place was frustration mixed with some anger, though he didn't seem to be directing it at her.

Angelique inhaled. "There is another realm besides Tarradon, Earth, and Cargonia. It's a closed realm where beings can't leave unless Fate decides it's best for the universe."

Interest sparked in his eyes for a moment but then was followed by doubt. "I don't understand."

"I'm not sure I can explain it very well. I was let out of this closed realm—for lack of a better term—and sent to Tarradon. Why? Because it is my goal to watch over the next generation of Guardians." She'd never mentioned that she knew who these Guardians were, and she hoped he didn't deny it. "I actually knew that both Chelsea and Kaleena were pregnant before they did."

Thane leaned back and chugged the rest of the wine. "You were sent to be a babysitter? Because I know you are my mate, I'm willing to admit that my family and the Caspians are Guardians, but you must be aware that we are the realms' protectors. We can protect the children ourselves."

Shit. He sounded pissed. His pride was getting in the way. "That's true, but even you and your family can't protect them against a dark entity."

He lifted his chin. "Declan and I fought against Sanditra and won."

As much as she didn't want to bruise his ego, he needed to understand. "Sanditra was a very powerful dark lighter—not a dark entity. There's a big difference. I'm sure Declan has mentioned that I intervened. If I hadn't, both of you would have died."

His eyes widened. "Declan said he was healed from the inside out and even heard your voice inside him when he went on the offensive, but I figured he was imagining things. He had been wounded pretty badly before his dragon healed him."

She shook his head. "He wasn't hallucinating. Because the situation was critical to my mission, I was able to send my white light into Declan. I healed him. His dragon didn't. That voice he heard was really me in his body directing him what to do. I shot white light into Sanditra, diluting her darkness. That was what crippled her. It was why Declan was able to kill her."

Thane looked away. It was almost as if she'd punched him in the gut. "I can't believe it."

"If I could spontaneously become white light right now to show you that I'm telling you the truth, I would, but I can only send my light through someone when Fate deems it necessary."

He lifted a hand and held up a finger. "Suppose I pretend what you say is fact."

"It is."

"Okay, then explain exactly what happened to Denalt. You said a dark entity overtook his body. How did he do it and why?"

"It's not like we're given a manual on these things, but just like my white light, its dark light can enter things—in this case humans. The light can bend around the cells in the body to get inside. It's the why of it all that I have yet to figure out."

"How can you be sure it was a dark entity? Was it because of the burn marks?"

"Yes. It wasn't until this happened that I became more certain than ever that a dark entity was even on Tarradon. I had sensed something bad inside Denalt, but I couldn't be positive he wasn't just a big bad dark lighter."

"I thought all dark lighters were bad," Thane said.

"They are."

"What else do you know?" Thane leaned closer.

"When the gates to my realm—if that is what they are even called—were opened up for me, I suspected one of them escaped too. I don't want to believe it was let out by Fate. That would be too cruel. If Fate let it out, what is its mission? And if it escaped using me as a conduit, what is the goal?"

"You would know better than me. Was yesterday the first time you felt him—or rather it?" Thankfully, Thane's question implied he was starting to believe her.

"It was the first time I was positive this dark entity was here. If Mange followed me to Thedia, he kept his distance. I never ran into him there, but there were a few times I thought I sensed him."

"His name is Mange?"

She waved a hand. "That's what I call him. His pure darkness is like a disease. It seemed to fit. He or she could be anyone really."

"Why were you sent to Thedia? The Sinclairs and Caspians are here."

"I wondered that too. It's not like we're told much before we are sent on our mission. My guess is that I needed a little seasoning first. My people skills were rather lacking. You all aren't the easiest species to understand."

He almost chuckled. "I agree with you on that."

"After a few months of watching and mimicking others, I realized it was time to head to Edendale. I know I was sent here for two purposes. One was to protect the children of the Guardians and the other was to find you."

He smiled briefly. "I'm glad you agree that we are mates."

"Yes, but let's not get sidetracked."

He held up a palm. "I totally agree. Let's start with the basics then. When were you born?"

Now it was her turn to chuckle. "I wasn't ever born in the usual sense. I don't have parents or siblings. I just was. My energy has been around for all eternity. Once I was put into my human form, my immortality ended. I will live as long as you once we have fully mated."

Thane stood, retrieved the rest of the wine, and carried it back over to the living room. "I think this is a three glass discussion."

Relief swamped her. "I'm actually astounded that you believe me."

"Trust me, I wouldn't have if Declan hadn't mentioned what happened to him during the fight with Sanditra. I mean, I saw him recover quickly, but I couldn't totally understand it. For the longest time, I thought he was making up the fact you'd been the one to heal him. I guess I need to thank you for saving his life. Apparently, Sanditra really did nearly kill us."

"If I hadn't interfered, she might have. I know you and your family have experienced all kinds of magic, but my magic is different—and more intense."

"Is that how you beat me on the obstacle course? By using magic?"

She wondered if he'd bring up his defeat on the second round. "No. I won using my own human talents."

The doorbell rang, and Thane jumped up. "Food's here."

Angelique was too distracted to eat, but she didn't want to give Thane any more reason to think she was some kind of freak. He paid the deliveryman and placed the food on the dining room table.

Angelique stood. "I'll get the silverware." This evening was turning out to be surreal. One minute she was telling him about being a light entity without a body, and the next she was setting the table as if they were some ordinary couple.

Once seated, they opened up the containers, scooped out their food, and dug into the meal, without saying much. She was sure he was trying to synthesize everything that she'd told him. It had to be overwhelming.

"Mmm. This is really good," she said, hoping to cut some of the tension in the air.

"I didn't think I was hungry, but I must have used up a lot of energy trying to understand everything."

She placed a hand on his. "Thank you for not telling me I'm crazy. I'm not sure how I could have shown you that I'm telling the truth. I just wish I had all of the answers."

Thane cut up his portion of the chicken Parmesan and wolfed it down. "Tell me what you know about this Mange dude. It might help us find him."

"I imagine he has a real name, but I don't know what it is. It's possible that when I was let out of the realm, Mange piggybacked on me. If Fate had let him out, why not give him a body?"

"I can't help you with that. The fact you didn't have a body until you were sent to our realm is beyond my mental abilities."

She waved a hand. "Let's forget about the logistics. After I *landed* on Thedia, I didn't run into Mange but that might have been because he hadn't figured out how to take over a body yet, so he kept his distance."

Thane set down his knife. "I find it hard to believe that Fate didn't swoop in and send him back to that closed realm—unless Fate meant for him to escape."

"It's possible, but why send him here? To cause a war? To spread a plague? It couldn't be to thwart me, as that would be highly counterproductive on Fate's part."

"How do we stop him?" Thane asked.

"That's the problem. I don't know," she said.

"Perhaps that is a third part of your destiny: stopping Mange."

Chapter Five

"I WISH I could be more certain about things," Angelique said, her fingers gripping her fork way too tightly. "If Fate wanted Mange stopped, why send him in the first place? Unless he really did escape."

Thane needed more information about this entity. "You said you sensed Mange inside of Denalt when he came to the mine. I wonder why I didn't sense anything evil radiating off him." Perhaps that scared him the most about all of this.

"His dark light sends out a certain vibe that resonates within me. It's more powerful than anything you would have ever experienced. Because it is different from a standard dark lighter's energy, you might not be trained to sense it."

Fuck. The Guardians were powerful creatures, filled with magic, but even if they worked together, they might not be able to take down this entity. "You said you've seen the charred exit wound once before? Where?" he asked.

"In Thedia." Angelique finished the last of her meal and then washed it down with the rest of her wine.

Thane tried to put the pieces together. "Let me get this straight. This Mange creature came here without a body. Needing someone, he found Denalt and entered him." He couldn't fathom it.

"More or less. How much Denalt was aware of what was happening, I don't know."

"Why did this being exit Denalt's body? It would call a lot of attention to himself."

Angelique glanced off to the side. "Most likely he sensed my awareness of his darkness. That means he'll continue to change bodies to avoid being found."

"And once he takes over a person, are they basically dead?" Thane's worst nightmare just came true.

"So it seems."

Thane tamped down his anger. "Do you know if it has a type? That is, could it inhabit a female's body just as easily? Will these hosts be around thirty years old like Denalt was, or might it take over an old man or a young child?"

She blew out a breath. "I don't know. I've only known these dark entities without bodies. It's not like we have parties and chat with them or hear rumors about their exploits."

"I'm sorry. I feel so helpless." Having lost his appetite, Thane pushed his plate away. "We need to do something."

"You mean I need to do something. You aren't equipped to kill him."

He didn't like that answer. "What can you do that I can't?"

"Shoot so much white light into him that it cancels out his darkness."

"You're positive that will work?"

"When I was in the realm, it wasn't like we went around trying to off each other. Sure, we battled a bit, and we communicated with each other in our own mental way, but without a physical form, it wasn't like we could hold a gun and shoot someone. When I sent my light through a dark entity, it slowed it down."

"Slowed, but not stopped?"

"Yes, but being in a body might make a difference." She tossed her napkin on the table.

"I'm sorry. I know this is hard for you, Angelique, but I'm overwhelmed with all these new ideas. Dark entities without bodies able to inhabit humans sounds rather far-fetched, but clearly it's true."

She grabbed the bottle of wine and emptied it into her glass. "I know. It's not like there is anyone I can ask either."

He snapped his fingers. "The Four Sisters of Fate might be able to help."

She shook her head. "Magnolia, Poppy, Primrose, and Acacia left yesterday on their two-week vacation. The shop is closed."

"Fuck. How can they do that in our time of need?"

"As good as they are, they might not have realized that Mange was on the loose. Or else they want us to figure it out for ourselves." She huffed out a laugh. "I never knew Fate was so cruel."

"So now what?"

"We wait for its next move," Angelique said.

"Which is?"

"It will find another body. As soon as I sense its presence, we'll go from there."

Thane shook his head. "I don't like it. If only I could tell a dark entity from a light one, I might know what to do."

She reached out and stroked his arm, setting his body on fire. "That's why I'm here."

"I do like the fact you are here as my mate." Thane tilted his head to the side.

"That's the best part." A genuine smile crossed her lips, lighting his scales.

"Maybe it's time we explore that purpose and see where it takes us."

CONFLICTING EMOTIONS ASSAULTED her. Angelique was put here in part to be Thane's mate, but she was given no time frame in which to actually mate with him. Even though it would be months before the babies were born, it would be foolish to become distracted by the hot Thane Sinclair. Perhaps Mange was put in her path to keep her focused.

On the other hand, every time Angelique was near Thane, her body betrayed her. Maybe if she indulged in her fantasy of sleeping with him, it would dispel the built-up lust, and she could get on with her mission. Yes, that seemed the most logical thing to do! Or was she rationalizing because she wanted him? Damned if she knew.

In hindsight, she should have stayed longer in Thedia in order to figure out human nature more fully.

"Angelique?" Thane asked.

Crap. She had to remember what he just said. Oh, yeah. He wanted to explore their attraction more fully. Or at least that was what she thought he said. "What do you have in mind?" Angelique wanted to be sure she hadn't misunderstood him.

Thane pushed back his chair, stepped over to her, and drew her to her feet. "For starters, let's try something more than those chaste goodbye kisses you've been giving me." His green eyes flashed teal as he grabbed a handful of her hair. "Oh, Angelique, you have no idea what you do to me."

Her indecision just flew out the proverbial window. From the way his gold scales illuminated his skin and how his eyes were flashing, she could tell the man was rather excited. Little did he know, his level of desire was about to grow a hell of a lot more. "Tell me."

"How about I show you instead?"

Heat poured through her body at his sultry comment. As if Fate had flung open the gates of passion, Angelique threw her arms around his neck and kissed him like she'd wanted to for a long time.

While she'd never allowed herself to just go with her gut before, this felt oh so right. Thane must have some white light inside him too because his energy lit her up from the inside. He cupped her cheek with one hand and drew her closer with the other. His talons had poked out of his fingertips a bit and were pressing into her skin.

When he ran his tongue along the seam of her lips, she welcomed him in. Every thought in her body fled as he plunged, tasted, and explored. As soon as his hard cock pressed against her stomach, a few warning bells went off in her head, but she refused to listen. His touch, his taste, his scent, and the way he held her with such care melted her resolve to keep her distance any longer. For once, she wanted to live in the moment. Everything about Thane Sinclair screamed hotness, dominance, and total desire.

He slipped his palms to her waist and then slid his hands under her shirt, his touch scorching her flesh and his talons slightly scratching her skin. As much as she wanted to take things slow, she couldn't. It was almost as if their energies had bonded, and they couldn't be separated if she tried.

Matching his urgent movements, she dragged her hands along his rippled back, pushing the fabric of his T-shirt upward.

He broke the kiss and then grunted. "I need you naked. I know you've been hesitant around me, Angelique, but I have to be honest. I can't keep away any longer."

Not only were his teal eyes swirling with flecks of amber, his gold scales were bright under his skin. One of his talons had fully poked through his hand. He stared at it and then hissed. His hand returned to normal.

"I can't either." When she pulled his shirt over his head and dropped it on the floor, her breath caught at his beauty. They'd run the obstacle course, but he'd been wearing a shirt. This was the first time she could admire him in all of his glory. "You're magnificent," she whispered.

He pressed a thumb to her lip. "I'm glad you think so, but I believe that honor belongs to you." His eyes then glazed over as he lifted off her shirt and brought the fabric to his face. His eyes closed for a moment as he inhaled her scent. "You're more beautiful than I ever imagined. And your aroma wakes up my dragon."

Wow. She was speechless. This was what it meant to be someone's fated mate. When Thane lowered his hands to her chest, Angelique stood frozen as he rubbed his thumbs over her white lace bra. Every cell inside her wanted his touch all over.

She reached around her back and unhooked the clasp. Thane then lifted his fingers to her shoulders. Slower than a glacier could move, he dragged down her straps until the cups edged over the tips of her breasts, allowing the bra to fall to the ground.

Leaning over, he flicked his tongue over the tip and groaned. The wonderful spikes of pleasure had her clasping his arms and digging her nails into his skin. Never before had she experienced such intensity. Sure, she'd felt joy and sensuality while in her light form, but nothing compared to this body-tingling pleasure.

Thane nipped and sucked on one breast while he gently kneaded the other. Angelique desired more. She reached between them and tried to undo the button on his pants, but he stopped her.

"Hold on," he said between strokes.

Damn him. It wasn't fair that he could tempt and tease her while she had to stand there. When Thane slightly bit her swollen nipple, her breast glowed white from within.

Angelique jumped back. "Did you see that?" she asked.

"The glow? Yes. Why?"

"I know dragons glow their scale color when excited, but I never have, mainly because I'm not a dragon."

He straightened and grinned. "Maybe it just means I've turned you on."

She wanted to smack him for his smugness, but at the same time, she didn't want him to stop what he was doing. Frustration made her ego and desire collide. "Let's just say I'm unsure what happened. I can't be certain if what you did excited me or not. Maybe you should try harder to turn me on." Angelique dragged a nail down his gloriously naked chest.

Thane barked out a laugh as his hand flew between her legs to cup her. "How's this?" He gave a gentle squeeze as he looked down at her.

The sudden thrill caused her to stand on her toes and grab hold of his shoulders. "Interesting choice," she croaked out.

Normally, Angelique was the aggressor but with Thane her emotions were short-circuiting her brain.

"Another kiss might do the trick," he said.

Thane leaned over, and what followed further blew her mind. Erotic thoughts swirled inside her, taking her places she'd never been—and that was from a kiss!

Heart pounding, she leaned back. "You need to get more naked too."

Without breaking eye contact, he toed off his boots, stepped back, and dropped his jeans.

Her eyes bulged at his jutting cock. "You go commando. Another interesting choice."

"I was in a hurry to get here."

To tell her that his friend had died? Or had he planned all along to seduce her? At this moment, Thane seemed to have put that horror out of his mind.

"Sweet." Before he could tell her to stop, she grabbed his hard shaft. Whoa. She was barely able to wrap her fingers around him, and that gave her pause—but only for a second.

Faster than she could move from her realm to his, he unlatched her hand and nodded to her slacks. "Your turn."

"Fine." Bending down, Angelique tugged off her boots and socks. Once done, she stood back up and unhooked her slacks. Just as she started to unzip them, Thane stopped her.

"Let me do that." The man certainly seemed to like to be the one in control. "And no touching me."

"What?" She immediately placed her hands on his chest. "Why not?"

Instead of answering, he tugged down her pants, sliding both her slacks and panties to her ankles. "Step out of them."

She debated whether to obey him or not, but Thane seemed to need to do it his way, so she did as he asked. Now they were both naked, and all she wanted to do was plaster her body against his.

His skin pulsed gold, and she'd never seen anything more beautiful. "Does it hurt?" she asked as she ran a finger over the different glowing spots.

"No, but it does make me warm." He returned her hand to his chest.

Heat radiated out in pulses. His cock hadn't changed colors, but she wanted to see if she could excite him enough to make it turn pure gold. Without asking permission, she dropped to her knees and drew his hardness deep into her throat.

He grabbed a handful of her hair and tugged. "Angelique! Be careful."

She had no intention of stopping. Keeping one hand on his hip, she cupped his balls with her free hand and squeezed slightly. Suddenly, he stepped out of her grasp, lifted her by the waist with one arm, and carried her to behind the couch that sat in the middle of the room. He set her down. "Stay bent over," he commanded as he lightly pressed on her back.

Her pussy swelled in anticipation. Gripping the sofa back, she stuck out her butt and then widened her legs. Even she could detect her sexual perfume.

Thane stepped right behind her and slipped his cock between her legs. "I want to taste you so much, but if I do, I won't last. Forgive me."

He reached around her body and cupped her breasts. Massaging them, he kissed her neck. Goosebumps raced up her body partly because she thought he might try to mate with her. At this moment in time, she wasn't ready.

Instead of pressing his now sharpened teeth into her skin, he licked her neck before dragging his wicked tongue up to the shell of her ear. "What you do to me," he whispered.

The tugging on the shell of her lobe, together with what his magic fingers were doing to her body, made Angelique fear she might combust too soon. That was all before he'd even entered her.

Wanting to hurry the inevitable, she reached as far as she could between her legs and stroked one side of his cock. "I need you."

"Give me a second," Thane said, his voice wavering.

Angelique might be a light entity, but when she wanted something, she went after it with gusto. She pushed back her hips, catching his cock between her wet folds.

"Angelique!"

His cry of desperation caused her arms to glow white. Holy shit. Nothing like that had ever happened to her before tonight. True, Fate might not have given her a lot of knowledge about her kind when in a human body, but Angelique never thought she'd experience a glow from within.

When she wiggled her butt once more, Thane pressed his sharp teeth against her neck, and she stilled.

"Please don't move like that anymore. It's too much and destroys my ability to keep control."

"Then please don't keep me waiting," she tossed back.

His dick found his target, and he drove into her hard. At that second, the lust and joy were so overpowering that she was certain she'd turn into light and float away.

"Yes!" She dug her nails into the sofa and lowered her forehead to the protruding pillow back.

"You are a goddess," Thane panted as he withdrew and pounded back into her.

She wasn't a goddess but she saw no harm in letting him think what he wanted. Right now, Angelique was doing everything in her power to keep her climax in check until his arrived.

As if he could read her thoughts, Thane pinched her nipples hard, bringing her back to the bliss at hand.

"Stop for a moment," she panted.

He froze. "What's wrong?" Concern colored his words.

As soon as Thane withdrew, Angelique flipped over. Keeping her legs spread, she leaned back against the sofa. "Now kiss me."

He grinned, and her heart melted. Their tongues tangled as his cock returned to its rightful place. Dragging her hands over his shoulders and down the small mountains he called biceps, she lifted her hips, meeting each of his thrusts. Heat built. Excitement overwhelmed her. Desperate to reach that pinnacle, she slid her hands around to his back and arched hers until their chests met.

Thane broke the kiss. "I can't hold out any longer."

"Me neither."

He closed his eyes and then dipped his head as their rhythm increased. With each thrust, she drew closer and closer to her orgasm. He dragged his teeth across her collar bone, only to capture her lips a moment later. It was the final straw. Her orgasm swooped in and claimed her hard.

A deep-throated groan escaped from Thane a second before his hot seed scorched her. Head spinning, she held onto him with all of her strength. His hand slipped under her butt, and then Thane withdrew. He lifted her up, and walked her around to the front of the sofa and set her down. "I'll get something to clean us up with."

"There are towels in the drawer to the right of the sink."

He tapped her nose and strode off, returning with a wet cloth a moment later. After cleaning her up, he wiped himself off, and then tossed it into the sink.

After catching her breath, Angelique managed to sit up. "That was incredible. In fact, it was so good, I don't think we should do that again for a very long time."

Chapter Six

THANE WAS SPEECHLESS. Angelique had to be kidding. "What do you mean you don't want to have sex with me again?" She better say it was a joke.

Angelique stood and paced in front of him. There was no way he could think straight with her naked. Hell. He'd just had the most mind-altering sex in his life, and she claimed she didn't want a repeat performance? How was that possible? Mates needed each other on an atomic level. From the way she wasn't looking at him though, she was serious.

"That's not quite what I said. We need to wait, that's all. The timing is wrong for a relationship."

Thane clasped her shoulders. "We are mates. Are we talking two days here? Two weeks? Or two months?"

Her lips pressed inward. "Until Mange is dead."

What sounded like a bark, burst out of his mouth. "That could take months."

"True, and if he continues like this, it might take longer than that. I don't want us to become distracted. We need to focus on getting rid of him."

Angelique was talking crazy. "Mange aside, I'm distracted when I'm not with you. I've been extremely patient about letting you decide when the time was right, but there is no way I can keep my distance any longer, especially after what just happened."

She stroked his face, her eyes full of sympathy. "I don't want to hurt you—or rather I don't want you to get hurt."

Now she was insulting him. "I'm the Guardian, remember?"

"And I'm a light entity, and as such, I'm the only one who stands a chance against this thing."

"How can you be so sure? You said you've never fought a dark entity while in your…your human form before."

She stepped out of his grasp, picked up her panties, and slipped them on. He would have stopped her, but it was for the best. Seeing Angelique naked prevented him from thinking rationally.

"I know. That's why I need to be careful around Mange," she said.

"Let me ask you this: If he takes over a dragon shifter's body, will he be able to fly?"

With her slacks in hand, she spun around. "I don't know for sure, but I'm thinking he can."

"Great." He snatched his jeans from the floor. "I'm telling the rest of the family. They need to be on high alert for this *thing*."

She nodded. "Just warn them to keep their distance."

"The problem is that I couldn't detect his dark signature. If no one else can, they won't be able to stay away either." He shoved his foot through one leg and then the other. Snatching his shirt off the floor, he pulled it over his head, his anger growing by the minute. "I need to let the others know right away."

"Do you want me to come with you?"

Part of him wanted her by his side at all times since he wasn't convinced she could completely protect herself. The ego half of his being wanted to do this by himself. After all, he was the one who trained the Guardians. He was the master fighter—not Angelique.

Thane studied her. Conflict swam in her eyes, as did a plea he couldn't resist. "I'd like that. I'm sure there will be questions I can't answer."

She nodded. "Do you think they'll freak when I tell them what I really am?"

"Declan sure won't be surprised. He'll confirm what you say is true."

"Then I guess I better get dressed."

While Angelique changed, Thane called his cousin, Anderson Caspian. As a police detective who often dealt with homicides, he needed to know what Edendale was up against. Angelique would ultimately be the one to decide just how much of this dark entity-light entity stuff she wanted the world to know about. He wondered if the coroner should be told that Denalt had been invaded by a dark entity too, or would Angelique restrict it to the Caspians and Sinclairs? So many questions—too few answers.

Humans knew about shifters, but their intimate knowledge of magic was limited. If they learned that an unstoppable evil force was out there, panic would ensue, making the Guardians' job that much more difficult.

After speaking with Anderson, he called Declan and asked him to round up as many Guardians as he could for an emergency meeting. No sooner had he disconnected than Angelique came out dressed in jeans and a tight-fitting navy blue T-shirt with matching sandals. Her usual bouncy step was gone. In its place appeared to be dread.

"Ready?" he asked.

"Yes. I guess I always knew this time would come when I had to expose my real self."

"You'll be fine. Everyone will be supportive. Just as a warning though, Anderson is going to meet us at the SinCas building too. It will give us more privacy if we meet there."

"Good."

"Drive or fly?" he asked.

"Drive."

She handed him her car keys and then grabbed her purse. Once he locked up her house, Thane held open her car door and she slid in. He hopped into the driver's side, started the engine, and pulled out of the driveway. "You have no idea what Mange is really doing here in Edendale?"

"No."

"I personally find it odd that he would want to be in the same province as someone who can take him down."

She let out a long breath as if to compose her thoughts. "Dark entities want to disrupt people's lives. From the moment we are aware, we are given knowledge of how things work. We understand good and evil. A white entity's goal is to do only good, while the dark entities want to create chaos. As for Mange's specific mission, I too, find it strange that he would come here. It must be to make sure I don't succeed."

"At what? Mating with me?"

She sucked in a breath. "I hope not that."

He glanced over at her, not liking the way her words faded away. "What aren't you telling me?"

"Nothing. I don't believe Fate will let Mange harm me, because it has a job for me to do."

Thane's fingers tightened on the wheel. "But?"

"Why follow me to Avonbelle when he had the whole realm to work in? Mange must want me to be aware that he's here or he wouldn't have gone to your mine. I figured if he wanted to kill you, he would have done so already."

"That's not all that reassuring. Can he walk through walls or something?"

"I can't, but no telling what Mange is capable of."

The SinCas building came into view, and because the jewelry store on the bottom floor was closed at this hour, there were a few empty spaces in front. After parking, Thane scanned the area for anyone who could be Mange.

He opened up Angelique's door. "Tell me if you sense anyone."

She looked around, studying the few people walking by. "I don't sense him."

Using his special scale to unlock the door adjacent to the jewelry store, they entered the building. "Everyone will be meeting us in the fourth floor conference room."

When he pressed the elevator button, the doors to each of the two shafts opened simultaneously. Spooky. Thane didn't remember that happening before. He motioned Angelique inside one of them, and then pressed the button for the fourth floor. It stopped on the third, and Griffin got in.

"Hey. What's the big meeting about?" his cousin asked.

"Angelique and I will be talking about a dark entity that is on the loose."

His brows rose. "Dark entity? That sounds ominous."

"It is."

Because the woman Thane suspected was Griffin's mate had been held captive by the dark lighter, Sanditra, Griffin would be interested in anything to do with such beings.

The elevator stopped on the fourth floor, and the three of them exited.

Just as they turned toward the conference room, a scream, along with the sound of the next elevator's cable coming loose, cut through the air.

"Holy shit," Thane said.

His mind raced. Whoever was in the elevator was not only trapped, they'd never survive the fall.

As calmly as she could be, Angelique stepped in front of the closed doors, placed her palms on the metal door, and closed her eyes. Two seconds later, the screeching sound stopped.

She faced both him and Griffin. "I put a spell on the elevator to stop it, but whoever is inside is still trapped."

Whoa. How could she put a spell on metal cables? No one he'd ever known could have done that other than maybe the Four Sisters of Fate. Now however wasn't the time to dig into her abilities.

Using his considerable strength, Thane pried opened the doors and looked down. "The elevator is between the first and second floor." He turned to Griffin. "Come on. We need to help whoever is in there. Angelique, stay here."

"Hell no."

He didn't have time to argue. She was one stubborn woman. "Fine, but we need to hurry."

The three of them took the stairs instead of using the remaining elevator. This had to be sabotage. Their maintenance of the SinCas building was impeccable. He knew because he was in charge!

When they reached the first floor, he and Griffin opened those elevator doors.

"Oh, thank goodness. I thought I was going to crash," Greer said in a voice that sounded eerily calm. Her composed attitude didn't surprise Thane even though she'd experienced a harrowing event.

Griffin's sister was slumped on the floor with her skirt hiked high on her thigh with one of her red shoes on the other side of the elevator. After the abrupt stop, she'd be bruised for sure.

Griffin reached in. "Give me your hands, and we'll help you out."

Greer did as she was asked, and a second later, she was on her feet, straightening her beige skirt. "Thank you." She looked between Thane and Griffin. "How did that happen?"

Griffin retrieved her other shoe and handed it to her.

Angelique grabbed Thane's arm. "He's here."

Thane stiffened. "Fuck. Where?"

The front door they'd come through slammed shut. "He's gone," she said with a determined look in her eye that implied Angelique was ready to go after him right now.

"How did he get inside in the first place? It doesn't matter. He did. I need to find him," Thane said.

"No! You're no match for him." Angelique was nearly shouting.

"I'll help," Griffin said. "We can take him down, but we'll have to hurry before he gets away."

Thane's shoulders sagged as reality struck. "Except we won't find him." He turned to Angelique. "Will we?"

She shook her head. "He could be sitting across the street sipping coffee, laughing at us right now. We have no idea what he looks like."

"If we check the security cameras, we'll be able to see him, assuming he didn't wear a mask," Griffin said.

Thane placed a hand on Griffin's shoulders. "The hunt will have to wait. Even if we see his face on camera, he might have changed it by now."

"Are you kidding me?" Griffin asked. His usually calm cousin appeared agitated and with good cause. The Guardians were born to seek justice.

"I wish I were. Let's head to the conference room. We'll try to explain everything." Thane turned to Greer. "Are you okay to join us?"

She straightened. "I wouldn't miss this for the world."

WHEN ANGELIQUE WALKED into the conference room, the place was packed, but she only recognized about half of them. Thane's hand to her back comforted her as he guided her over to the large wooden table where four seats remained vacant.

Thane pulled out a chair for her. "Sit here."

He dragged out the chair next to hers but remained standing behind it. Griffin and Greer sat at the far end. Finn, Declan, Nessa, and Kaleena were also there. The other four people she didn't know. Thane introduced her to each of them.

"I asked Anderson here because there's been a homicide," Thane said.

"You said you know who did this? What can you tell us?" Anderson asked.

For the next fifteen minutes, Thane gave an accurate detailing of how Denalt had been infected with a dark entity and why he'd died. "We don't completely understand what we are up against, but only Angelique seems to be able to identify him."

"I know from experience that you are a very powerful white lighter," Declan said, "but the way Thane describes this Mange guy, he seems similar to you—other than the fact you do good and he does bad."

Angelique pushed back her chair and stood. "Declan is right. I'm different from your traditional white lighter. I'm a white entity." Her hands shook as she described where she came from and why.

"Can you turn into white light at will?" Declan asked. "Because that's what it felt like when you were inside me."

"No. Fate decides when I can do that. Chelsea and her baby were in danger, which was why Fate allowed me to intervene."

"So you're here to protect my baby and Chelsea's?" Kaleena asked with her eyes wide.

"Yes."

A ton of questions followed until Thane intervened. "Let's not get sidetracked. We had an incident just moments ago." He explained about the elevator sabotage.

"I thought I was going to be severely injured since the elevator was too small for me to shift," Greer said, her voice suddenly shaking. "While a fall of thirty feet wouldn't have killed me, I wouldn't have relished the pain of a few broken bones."

"Are you thinking it was a warning of some sort?" Jamison Sinclair said as he moved his gaze between Thane and Angelique.

She held up her hand, indicating she would field that question. "Mange—my name for this dark entity—has a hidden agenda. Even if we look at the security tapes and find this man, if you attempt to capture him, Mange will exit that body and leave the man dead, only to enter another."

"Fuck," Anderson said. He was glancing down at his phone. He looked up. "Sorry. That was the station. Seems you are right. Apparently, another man with the same burn mark in his chest was found two blocks from here."

Noise from the group erupted. Finally, Thane had to pound the table for quiet. "I don't want anyone to think they can hunt this guy down and kill him."

"We'll travel in pairs," Griffin said.

Angelique wasn't getting across to them. "The only way to kill him is to infuse him with my white light. The problem is that I can't be sure I possess enough to totally destroy him."

"What if I add mine to yours?" Kaleena asked.

Thane's sister was so sweet. "Not on your life. That might be exactly what Mange hopes will happen. My goal is to protect your child, and I won't jeopardize your baby for any reason."

Chapter Seven

GIVEN THE TIMING of the attack, Thane was pretty sure Mange was behind it all. What he couldn't figure out was why attack an elevator? Had Mange meant to mess with the one Thane, Angelique, and Griffin had been in? Thane could have chosen the other elevator just as easily.

Shit. He had no idea what a fall of that kind could have done to Angelique if she'd been the one inside. She didn't possess the ability to shift and heal herself. His gut twisted at the ramification of the near catastrophe.

"I want to see the body for myself," Thane announced.

"Why?" Angelique asked.

"I want to make sure Mange caused this man's death."

Anderson waved his phone. "My coroner claims the wounds looked similar." He stood and shoved his phone in his pocket.

"I'd still like to see him." Thane pushed back his chair.

Angelique followed suit. "I'm coming with you."

He wanted her by his side at all times—for both of their safety. "Good idea. Griff? You want to join us?" While his cousin wasn't a white lighter, he possessed other talents that would be useful. Between the three of them, along with several members of the police department, Mange should keep his distance.

"Sure."

When the four of them arrived at the scene, the body was covered with a white sheet. Anderson jogged toward the coroner and asked to see the corpse. Thane followed right behind but not before pleading with Angelique to stay put. For once she agreed.

When the coroner pulled back the sheet, the evidence was irrefutable, except this time, instead of exiting from the middle of his chest, the entity left through the man's face. Thane's gut churned at the horror. The poor soul. Now more than ever, Thane was truly scared for the people of Edendale.

"Do you have an identification?" Anderson asked the coroner.

The doctor shook his head. "No. He had no wallet or any form of identification on him. We took prints, but it will take a while to process them."

Anderson motioned Thane off to the side. "This is worse than I could ever imagine."

"I know." If Angelique ever went against this guy, Thane feared he might destroy her. "So far, both victims have been human. Not that I'm suggesting a dragon shifter could take him down, but I'm thinking he'd have some kind of advantage." At least Thane wanted to believe that was true.

"Let's hope," his cousin said.

After asking a few other questions, Thane returned to Angelique. "I think I should take you back. It's been a long day."

"It was the entity's doing, wasn't it?"

"I'm afraid so."

Griffin turned to Angelique. "Thanks for being so forthcoming about what you are. That took a lot of guts. We might have gone in blind against this entity if you hadn't warned us. Some of us could have died while trying to take him down."

"I'm happy to help. I'm not sure if any amount of warning would help the ordinary person."

"Probably not." Griffin turned to Thane. "I'm going to stop by Danita's place. While her white light power is slowly returning after her experience with Sanditra, I want to warn her to be careful. No telling who this Mange will want to harm next."

Angelique placed a hand on Griffin's arm. "If it's any consolation, I don't think he wants to mess with white lighters. They can do him some harm."

"I'll keep that in mind."

All during the drive back to Angelique's house, she remained quiet. "You're really worried, aren't you?" Thane asked.

She twisted in her seat toward him. "Of course. I'm torn too. I'm the only one who can stop him, and yet I fear I may not be strong enough to end his existence. I'm really worried for everyone on Tarradon."

Thane worked to keep his anger in check. "Isn't there some trap we can set for him?"

"Like what? Have him walk into a field of explosives and blow him up? Or trap him at the bottom of a mine and collapse it?"

That was exactly what he was thinking. "Maybe."

"I wish it were that simple. Mange would leave whatever body he was occupying and slide out of wherever he was trapped. Normal light might travel in straight lines, but our light can bend."

She painted a dim picture. "Great."

Thane pulled into her driveway. As much as he wanted to comfort her, Thane wanted to honor her wish for them to keep their distance for a while. Though after what just happened, he wasn't sure he could.

He rushed to her side to help her out. They were halfway to her front door when she held out his hand to stop him.

"I sense something." Her whole body shook.

"Get inside," he commanded.

"You get inside."

Thane couldn't help but laugh, though he was well aware the situation was not funny in the least. Angelique was capable of a lot, but he'd die first before he let her tackle this dark entity alone.

A man emerged from the side of her house and smiled. "Well, well, Angelique. We meet again."

Thane didn't recognize him, but the unknown man could be a customer of hers.

She stepped forward, but Thane stopped her before she moved too close to him. "What do you want, Mange?"

Thane had to force his dragon not to attack. Timing was the key to taking him down.

"Mange? Is that my new name? How cute."

Angelique wisely didn't answer. "You need to leave," Thane said, stepping in front of Angelique. "Now."

The man scowled. "This is between Angelique and me."

She puffed out her chest. "What do you want?"

"For you to stop interfering. Fate has given me a job to do."

"And what job is that?" she asked.

The creepy man smiled. "Something you won't like."

"How do you expect me to stop doing something if you don't tell me what it is?"

Thane had enough of this asshole. He shifted into his dragon form and shot upward, positive he could protect Angelique even from a height of fifty feet. Just as he was about to blow out a stream of fire, Mange also shifted into a dragon. Shit. While that came as a surprise since he hadn't sensed the man was a shifter, it worked for him. After all, no one was a better fighter than Thane Sinclair.

Thane instantly went on the offensive, shooting higher, and then stopping without notice. Sure enough, Mange came after him. Fool. Thane swung his tail back and forth to gain momentum. Even though Mange was a dark entity, he wouldn't be skilled in fighting like a dragon.

Once his enemy was close enough, Thane whipped his tail around Mange's arms, preventing him from clawing out Thane's heart. Mange struggled. To Thane's surprise, Mange managed to free himself. Damn. He was a strong bugger. Mange shot out a rather weak blast of fire that Thane dodged. This monster's life had to end.

Thane executed a quick maneuver to attack from the underside. As if Mange had the same idea, he flipped around, coming snout to snout with him. This was going to be a bit more challenging than Thane first thought.

Thane extended his claws and shot toward Mange. Before the dark entity could react, Thane dug his talons into the dragon's chest.

His attacker's mouth opened and a pathetic puff of fire escaped. The dark entity's wings fluttered as he tried to keep aloft but failed.

Not wanting to be taken down with him, Thane let go and joyfully watched as the limp dragon floated to the ground. Thrilled that he'd killed the biggest threat to Tarradon in a long time, he let out a burst of fire that was sure to impress Angelique.

When Thane dipped his head to return to the ground, his heart nearly stopped. The dragon was sprawled out on the ground. A human's body had taken its place, indicating the dragon was dead. What nearly froze every muscle in his body was the sight of Angelique collapsed next to him.

The instant he landed, Thane shifted and rushed over to her. He dropped to his knees. "Angelique!"

When she didn't respond, he scooped her up and pressed her warm body to his chest. Her heart was still beating, but her breathing came out so slowly he feared she would die. Only then did he notice that the man on the ground had a burned hole in his back. "Shit."

With some effort, Thane scooped up her purse and rushed her to the front door. Holding Angelique in his arms, he worked to locate her door key. Once inside, he set her on the sofa and then rushed to pour her a glass of water. How he thought that would help he didn't know, but it was all he could think of to do.

Thane placed the full glass on the coffee table and sat on the edge of the sofa. "Angelique, baby, can you hear me?"

He studied her mouth, her eyes, and her fingers for any signs of movement, but found none. Fearing the dark entity had entered her, he lifted her shirt. When he spotted no discoloration, he heaved a sigh. If the entity hadn't taken over her, why wasn't she waking up? His hand shook as he stroked her cheek. Her temperature felt normal to the touch, so what was wrong with her? "Angelique, sweetheart, open your eyes."

Come, on, come on, he mentally urged. Damn it. The fight might have been a ploy by this entity to separate them.

His mind finally cleared. Declan was a healer. Thane bet his brother would know what to do. He yanked the phone from his pocket and dialed him.

"What did you find out? Was the dead man taken over by the dark entity?" Declan asked.

Thane forgot that he hadn't spoken with him yet. "Yes, but that's not why I'm calling. The dark entity hurt Angelique. We're at her place. Can you help her?"

"I can go to her, but she'd be better off at the safe house."

Shit. He hadn't been thinking. "You're right. I'll fly her there now. Meet me at the mine." Thane disconnected before his brother could answer.

If she needed something else to wear when she awoke, he'd come back for it. "Time to go, Angelique. We need to get you someplace safe."

It took a bit of lifting and then setting her down, but eventually, Thane managed to take off with her in his grasp. Probably because of the stress, his heart was beating erratically by the time they arrived at the mine. He'd constantly searched the skies for someone who could be Mange in disguise but encountered no one. Never before had Thane met anything so vile.

Once he landed, he rushed inside with her to where Declan was waiting. "Tell me what happened," his brother said.

As Thane carried Angelique into the bedroom where he would stay when he used the safe house, he explained how the dark entity had shifted into a dragon after Thane had. "The battle was swift and decisive. It probably lasted less than three minutes. I watched him plummet straight down to the ground after I'd managed to stab his heart with my talon." Thane set her down on the bed.

"Did you see the dark entity attack Angelique?"

Guilt assaulted him. "No. I was congratulating myself for killing this evil force and didn't think to watch Angelique. When the dragon limply sailed downward, I believed I'd vanquished him. In retrospect, the dark entity must have left the body before the shell of the dragon reached the hard ground."

"Did you check her for any injuries?" Declan asked in his professional tone.

"Yes, but I couldn't find any."

"She hasn't responded at all?" Declan asked.

"No."

His brother nodded. "Why don't you fix me a coffee, and I'll check out Angelique?"

Thane knew what his brother was doing—getting him out of the way. Not that he blamed him. Thane would hover, which would distract him. "Be right back."

"Take your time."

Thane rushed into the kitchen, reliving the entire evening, from the sabotage on the elevator to this dark entity finding them at Angelique's house. She'd sworn that if she infused this entity with her white light that she could destroy him—or at least turn him away. So how had he gotten the drop on her? Surely, she would have sensed his presence. Or did this entity possess the ability to cloak his darkness just like Thane and the rest of the Guardians could cloak their dragon signature? If that were the case, Mange was even more dangerous than he'd first appeared to be.

Thane pounded a fist on the kitchen counter. If anything happened to Angelique, he would never forgive himself. Maybe it would have been better if he hadn't fought the evil creature at all. She might still be safe.

In hindsight, Thane had to assume it had been a ploy to get him away from her. Come to think of it, the dark entity hadn't put up much of a fight.

Thane made the coffee and headed back to Angelique and Declan. Balancing both drinks in one hand, he opened the door with the other. When he walked into the room, he half expected her to be sitting up and chatting away. Unfortunately, that wasn't the case.

Thane set down the drinks. "Any progress?"

Declan stood. "No. I can't get a reading on her either. There doesn't appear to be anything wrong with her. I'm guessing that this

Mange's darkness is attempting to shut something down, but I can't sense what it is."

"Fuck. Can't you do one of your spells?"

"I've tried."

"What about asking Greer to help?"

Declan shook his head. "I can call her, but I don't think she can do anything. What about the Four Sisters of Fate? If Angelique is your mate, they will help."

"Angelique said the sisters are on their annual vacation this week and next."

Declan glanced at the ceiling. "That really sucks."

"Tell me about it. Just in case they haven't all left, I'm going to check."

"Good idea," Declan said. "I'll try a few other things, but I'm not hopeful. Just hurry."

The worry in his brother's voice scared the living daylight out of him. "What are you saying?"

"Nothing. Now go."

Thane raced out of the underground shelter, shifted, and took off for the Four Sisters Pottery Shop. He almost missed the location because all the lights were out both in the store and in the back where the sisters lived.

He landed, shifted, and ran to the front door. A sign stated the shop would be closed for two weeks, but he refused to believe all four of them would be gone at the same time. He knocked on the store front door and rang the bell, expecting one of the sisters to open up. Only no one did.

"Damn it."

It was true. They were gone. He didn't want to believe that Angelique and he were on their own. There had to be someone who could help her. Flying as fast as he could, he made it back to the Sinclair Mines in short order, praying Declan had been able to unlock the mystery of whatever was happening to Angelique.

Racing back inside, Thane pushed open the bedroom door. "The

Four Sisters really are on vacation," Thane said, not believing the incredible strain in his voice.

"There's only one solution then," Declan said.

"What?"

"I need to go to Earth and ask Ophelia to come here."

"Who's Ophelia?"

"You remember: I mentioned her. She's the goddess from Earth who asked me to help her draw out an evil spell from one of their own."

"Ah yes. You met Chelsea on that trip."

"I did." Declan waved a hand. "Ophelia is also the Four Sisters of Fate's grandmother, and she owes me a favor."

Thane didn't understand any of it, but if she could help Angelique, he was all in favor of it. "What should I do while you jet on down to Earth?"

"Stay by Angelique's side and talk to her. Let her know she's not alone."

"Then go and godspeed."

Chapter Eight

A NGELIQUE WAS BACK in her light realm—or at least it felt like she was there. Did that mean she'd failed to protect the children of the Guardians, and Fate had recalled her? Images floated in and out of her mind's eye—Thane's teal eyes, his hand caressing her cheek, and his beautiful smile. His face seemed to come closer, yet when he opened his mouth, no words came out. Or was it that she just couldn't hear him?

Angelique had to be dreaming, which meant she needed to wake up. Only she couldn't. Looking around, all she saw was something that looked like dark webbing. When she reached out to touch it, a flash of white light abounded. Whoa. What was that? When no pain followed, she tried again, but this time nothing happened. Her mind spun at the conflicting input.

Glancing downward, she panicked when she was unable to see her body. What was happening to her? She expected her heart to race at this new turn of events, but nothing seemed to be beating. Oh, no. She had to be back in her realm. Only why?

"Angelique?" came a voice that appeared to be far away. At least there was sound to this internal movie.

She wanted to answer that she was there, but without a mouth, she couldn't respond. Mentally, she sent a message into the universe, but the person didn't call her name again. Please let this be an illusion and not her forever reality.

Not willing to give up so easily, Angelique tried to teleport around the realm like she used to, but the scene in front of her remained the same. Before she could figure out what was happening, a slow burning sensation overtook her worry. The intensity grew, as did the brightness around her. The dark webbing lightened and then burned, as if someone was trying to reach her with light—beautiful warm light.

"I'm here," she tried to communicate. Instead of an answer, the shafts grew brighter.

Pressure formed around where she believed her mind to be—or was she remembering what it was like when she was human?

A memory finally broke through. Mange had done this to her, whatever *this* was. From deep inside her, determination welled. She wasn't going to let him win.

A tremor suddenly shot through her as if there had been one of those realm earthquakes she'd heard about but had never experienced. Angelique tried to shoot her light out to let others know she was there, but nothing happened.

"Angelique."

She stopped fighting. That voice. It belonged to Thane. Yes, it was Thane's. Her mate. It was one of the reasons why she'd been sent to Tarradon. But why couldn't she answer him?

More warmth poured into her, and her mind fuzzed. Then nothingness encased her once more.

"WHY ISN'T SHE waking up?" Thane asked. He shouldn't be so impatient. Spells took time, but Ophelia was a goddess, or so Declan claimed.

Thane had never met one face-to-face before and had to admit he was a bit disappointed. This woman was old—as in ancient looking—yet Declan swore she had amazing powers.

Ophelia looked up at him. "It takes time. I can sense that Angelique is strong. She just needs to find her way back here."

"But she'll be able to, right?"

Declan clasped his shoulder. "Chill. We're doing our best, or rather Ophelia is doing her best. Apparently, your Mange person managed to send enough dark light into her to disrupt her essence."

"What the fuck does that mean?" Thane asked not caring that his words might be offensive to Ophelia.

Declan scrunched his brows. "You know that even our dragons take time to heal us."

This was different. This was Angelique. "I know, but I need her healthy again."

Angelique groaned, and Thane rushed to her side. Ophelia and Declan stepped back to give him room. He picked up her hand and squeezed it. "Angelique, can you hear me?"

When her fingers pressed into his palm, he almost wept for joy. Thane looked up at two hopeful faces. "She knows I'm here."

It wasn't long before Angelique finally opened her eyes, but she didn't seem to recognize him.

"It's me, Thane." Her tongue peeked out to wet her lips. Declan handed him a glass of water, and Thane lifted it to her lips. "Try to drink this."

To his delight, she was able to take a sip. "What happened?" she asked a minute later.

Relief rushed through him. "Mange did something to you."

She tilted her head to the side and then looked back at him. "I don't remember a lot."

"That's okay. You're with us now."

Her gaze focused on Ophelia. "Do I know you?"

"I'm Ophelia, and I live on Earth, but Declan thought I could help. Some dark entity put a curse on you, but I was able to break it up. You'll be good to go in no time, but I beg you not to engage with him again. I can't promise you'll recover a second time."

Thane didn't like hearing that.

Angelique reached up and squeezed the old lady's hand. "Thank you."

"You're welcome. I'll ask Declan to escort me home now. Good luck with this Mange being."

Thane wished she'd stay in case something else happened, but it was enough that she made the trip in the first place. It had to have been hard on her.

When the two of them were alone, he fluffed the pillow behind Angelique's head. "How are you feeling?" he asked.

Angelique tried to sit up, and he had to help her. Never had he seen her this weak before. "I'm not sure. I thought I was back in the entity realm where I swear I didn't have a body, yet I couldn't teleport like I could before."

"Do you feel any pain?"

Her lips pressed together. "Not really."

"What can you tell me about what you do remember?" He worked not to become angry that she let Mange get the drop on her.

"I was watching you fight Mange. I would have interfered if you had been injured and couldn't continue, but you seemed to have everything under control."

"I did. Or at least I thought I did."

"You'd flown under the dragon, extended your claws, and then stabbed him in the chest. I remember smiling and cheering. Then it was like I had been run over by a truck—not that I would really know what that felt like—but it was bad."

"You didn't see this guy then?"

She shook her head. "I assumed Mange was in the dragon's body. Even entities have to obey the laws of physics while we're here. We can't be in two places at once."

His mind whirled. "Maybe I wasn't fighting Mange at the end." Damn. He should have sensed the difference.

"When Mange's darkness tried to enter me, I fought hard to block him. I sent out what white light I could, but his darkness overpowered me. I'm betting mine was forceful enough though to do some harm. He might be recovering now too."

His Angelique was so brave. He cupped her face. "I'm just glad you're okay."

"Me too. Only now am I feeling my full light returning."

"I couldn't be happier," he said. Angelique swung her legs over the side of the bed. "What are you doing?"

"I feel fine. I'd like to go home."

He expected this stubborn streak. "It would be better if you stayed here for a few days."

An almost delighted look crossed her face. "And you? I hope the big, bad Guardian isn't going to take on Mange all by himself."

"Don't be silly. I plan to avoid him."

"How do you intend to do that? Even at the mines, he can find you."

He wished she didn't keep punching holes in his theory. "How about we go away together then—just the two of us? What do you say?"

Images of them swimming in a warm lake surrounded by nature and then making love while on the sandy banks, thrilled and excited him.

She better say yes. His dragon flashed his scales, hoping to convince her.

She cupped his face. "You are such a sweet man. I would love nothing more than to spend time alone with you, but that is the worst thing we can do. He'd find us for sure. If Mange tracked me to Edendale, he can find us anywhere."

Thane jumped up from the bed and paced, trying to come up with a plan. "I have another idea then."

"Don't say you want me to stay here while you go about doing your job, because I have a business to run too."

"I wish you would stay, but I know you. If I left you here, you'd sneak out. No, I was thinking of seeking help from someone who possesses quite a lot of magical power."

"The only ones who could help us are out of town, which means we need to avoid Mange for two weeks until the Four Sisters return."

"And you think Mange will be that patient?" he asked.

Angelique stood and eased over to him. Her hair was mussed, but she'd never looked more beautiful. "Not normally, but I have a feeling he's not doing so well right now. If that's the case, how about we enjoy each other while we have the chance?"

Thane hadn't expected the invitation. Not only had they made love earlier this evening, Angelique said she wanted them to keep their distance. "You know I'll always say yes, but why the change of heart?"

She dragged a seductive finger down his chest. "Almost dying has a way of changing a person's mind."

"I like it, but can you swear to me that you've fully recovered?"

She grinned and more than just his scales flashed. "I'm one-hundred percent. Ophelia and Declan are miracle workers. Thank you for asking them here," she said.

The seriousness of the situation reappeared. "I couldn't let anything happen to you." If Thane had told her what he was really feeling—that he was fast falling in love with her—she would balk and possibly push him away even more.

"I appreciate that." She moved a little closer. "So, what are we going to do about all of your excitable scales?" Angelique licked her lips, stood on her toes, and dragged his bottom lip between her teeth.

Lust grabbed him so hard, his knees almost buckled. "I did just fight that dragon."

"I know, and you were magnificent."

"Thank you, but the point is that I should probably clean up. Care to join me?"

"What will I put on after we shower? I don't have any other clothes."

She was being silly, and that turned him on. "I like to sleep naked," he said, barely able to contain his dragon from making an appearance.

"Me too. How about showing me the way?" Angelique asked.

When he led her to the bathroom, he eyed the tub and then the shower. His mind went wild debating which one was more romantic. "How about a bath? I'd light candles if I had any."

"Candles are overrated." She looked over at the oversized tub. "I think it's big enough for the two of us."

"It is." He closed the stopper and turned on the water. If only he'd known his mate would be there, he would have purchased some bath salts for her.

Wanting to do the honor of undressing Angelique, Thane lifted off her pullover and dropped it on the bathroom floor. "I remember this little number." He ran a finger over the top of her cute lacy bra. "Let me take it off this time."

Thane reached around Angelique's back and unhooked the clasp. As he lowered the straps, his breath caught at her beauty. Not able to wait until they bathed, he suckled on her breast while he plucked the other nipple with his fingertips. Blissful shards speared him, igniting his scales once more.

Apparently, Angelique wasn't willing to just stand there. She fumbled with his jeans, forcing Thane to step back.

"I need to ditch the shoes first," he said. He'd already removed hers after he placed her on the bed.

"Now the shirt," she commanded once he'd removed them.

Thane grinned. "Yes ma'am. I see you are back to your usual bossy self. That's a good sign." He finished stepping out of his jeans.

She planted a hand on her hip. "I am not bossy."

If he expected to make love with her after washing up, he better keep his mouth shut. All he could do was motion that he would zipper his lips.

"Funny," she said, acting like nothing traumatic had happened to her. She removed the rest of her clothes.

Thane tested the water. "It's perfect. Need help getting in?"

"Nope." She lowered her chin, sat on the edge, and swung her legs over the side. Once she was submerged up to her chest, Thane moved across from her, and the added mass nearly made the water spill over the tub's lip.

He lifted her foot, grabbed a bar of soap from the indented shelf, and washed her insole.

"That tickles," Angelique said as she tugged out of his grasp.

"I never would have guessed. Okay, change of plans." Instead of dragging the bar from toe to heel, he soaped up his hands first, and then massaged her foot.

She leaned her head back and smiled. "I could get used to this."

"I'm always up for touching and loving you."

Her eyes shot open. "Do you always have sex on your mind?"

"Don't you?" he returned. "It's how mates are supposed to react to each other."

She glanced to the side, acting as if he'd made her uncomfortable. "Yes, and that seems to be the problem. I was so enamored with watching you fight that I lost focus with my surroundings."

Damn. Here he'd thought she understood that she couldn't have stopped what had happened. "If you had known he was coming after you, what would you have done differently?"

She bit down on her lip, and his dick hardened even more. "I don't know. I didn't shoot my white light up at you both when you were fighting for fear of possibly distracting or even hurting you. When he came at me with his darkness, I reacted quickly, but I was too late to be effective."

"There you go. Shit happens. Even if you hadn't been distracted, you might not have been able to stop him."

"Maybe." She lifted the first foot again, and Thane repeated the cleansing massage.

Needing more contact, he lifted onto his knees and straddled her. While it probably wouldn't do much good, he lathered his palms and then washed her tits. She giggled again.

"How about taking this to the bedroom?" he suggested.

"Not before I do this." Angelique slipped the bar from the ledge, lathered her hands, and then grabbed his cock that was half submerged underwater.

"Whoa." She stroked him hard and fast. Even the warm water couldn't prevent his balls from contracting. "Okay, it's time to rinse."

"You're no fun," she said.

"You'd have been sorry if I'd let you continue. I'm sure you can use your imagination as to what could have happened."

"Eww." She then laughed.

Thane stood, removed the handheld showerhead off the wall and turned it on. After a final wash and rinse, he motioned for Angelique to stand. "Your turn," he said.

Angelique rose and lifted her arms. "Have at me."

She was such a tease, and he loved everything about her. "You have recovered, haven't you?"

"I'll let you be the judge of that in a moment."

"I can't wait."

Chapter Nine

MAYBE IT HAD been her near death experience, but Angelique was beyond turned on. Her need for Thane knew no bounds. After she washed and rinsed, Thane lifted her out of the tub. Never had she been treated so well. As soon as he set her down on the bath mat, Angelique grabbed a towel and began drying him off while he nabbed the other one off the towel warmer.

"Two can work faster than one," he said with a sly smile.

"I couldn't agree more."

She was thankful he was willing to forget about the horror of the day and just let them have another wonderful, mind-blowing experience. The release would help block the reality and ugliness that existed outside.

"Hey, focus," he said with a lot of cheer in his voice.

"What was I doing?"

"You missed a spot. Let me dry you first, and then you can do me."

That wasn't fair, but Thane seemed to need to make sure she was okay. His protectiveness was unnecessary, but she enjoyed how he wanted to take care of her. "Works for me."

Starting with her back, Thane dragged the towel over her shoulders and then along her spine. He knelt behind her and dried her butt for way too long.

"You are so beautiful," he said with so much awe that it embarrassed her.

"So are you."

He chuckled. "You can't see me."

"I have a good imagination." Before he'd finished drying her second leg, she flipped around. "You're taking too long."

He stood. "Is that so?"

"Yes. My nipples were getting cold."

His tongue pressed against his cheek. A second later, he bent over to encircle one tip with his tongue while his hand massaged the other. She groaned at the pleasure soaring through her. Wanting more, she grabbed his cock.

"If you make him explode, I'll have to take another shower, and that will delay the inevitable."

"Then how about we take this to the bedroom where we can feast on each other in a more comfortable setting?"

"I believe I suggested it first."

Angelique lifted her chin. "It wasn't the right timing back then."

"Uh huh."

Thane dropped the towel and swept her up into his arms. She wrapped one arm around his neck and rested her cheek on his damp chest. When they fell onto the bed, he made sure to cushion her from his weight.

"You gave me quite a scare, my pretty white entity."

"*You* had a scare? I was incredibly distraught when I heard your voice but couldn't reach you."

He stroked her cheek. "Let's make sure that never happens again."

"Let's hope. Since life is short, I want to make the most of it."

Thane kissed her nose. "Now you're talking."

Just when she thought he'd kiss her silly, he slid between her legs and held them open with his hands, his fingers pressing hard on her upper thigh. Lust swamped her even before the first swipe of his tongue. When he eventually licked her clit, she pressed her feet against the mattress to make her rear lift off the bed. Her body pulsed white light, and her heartbeat quickened.

Angelique clamped her hands on his head, holding on for dear life. Each swipe took her higher and higher. It was because of her brush with death, coupled with the wonderful way Thane treated her that she failed to hold back her climax. Her breath whooshed out, and her whole body coiled tight. When the initial rush passed, she collapsed onto the bed.

"That was a fast one," he said.

That sounded like a challenge, and Angelique never turned one down. "Okay, cowboy, let's see how long you last. On your back."

"I never say no to a lady."

"I need to warn you that I'm like no lady you've ever seen before."

"You've got that right." Thane flipped onto his back while she dropped down on her side, her feet near his head. No one said a woman couldn't have back-to-back climaxes.

The moment she grabbed his dick, he dragged her on top of him, his mouth pressed against her pussy, and her lips dangerously close to his dick. Angelique had definitely landed in the most amazingly heavenly realm. Leaning on one elbow, she grabbed his shaft as she went down on him. With each swirl of her tongue, her heat built. As much as she wanted to fully concentrate on what she was doing, when Thane slipped a finger inside of her, she nearly exploded again.

Angelique tightened her grip on his cock as he wiggled one, and then two, fingers inside her. Waves of delight spread throughout her so fast she had a hard time not screaming his name. His tongue replaced his fingers, and the walls came tumbling down as yet another climax swooped in. If he kept this up, she'd be too weak to have deep penetrating sex.

Now it was her turn to weaken his resolve, which meant she planned to excite him to the point of exhaustion. She drew him deep into her mouth while she pumped her fist hard and fast.

"Fuck, that feels amazing! I need to be inside you now," he commanded.

Wanting—or rather needing—the control after her harrowing experience, Angelique let go, spun around, and mounted him. His eyes widened as she slid right down onto his huge cock. The wave of slight discomfort from his big size surprised her, but the moment she lifted up and dropped back down, all was forgotten.

Thane slid his hands behind her back and drew her forward. Lifting up slightly, he took a swollen nipple in his mouth. "Mmm."

The divinely lustful pleasure was surpassed when he thrust upward, driving his cock to the hilt. Incredible bliss engulfed her, and she raised her head to give him more access to her breasts. He switched to the other side just as she rose and then plunged down on him. Her pussy walls clamped onto him, and she held on tight.

Thane slid his hand upward and drove his fingers into her hair. He drew her closer, tilted his head back a little, and kissed her as if there were no tomorrow. Angelique blocked out everything, pretending for the moment that they were the only two people in the universe. Water, or maybe sweat, slickened both of their bodies. With total abandon, she fucked him hard and fast.

Thane broke contact. "Angelique!"

He dragged his mouth to her neck. If he did mate with her, she wouldn't mind, but she'd always dreamed of her mate telling her he loved her first. "Thane, yes," she cried out.

With two more pumps, they both exploded. Her climax caused her white light to nearly encompass them both. It wasn't like anything she'd ever seen before.

As Thane's hot seed poured into her, she felt so complete she was unable to move. Her mind spun, and then everything went black. A moment later, Thane was returning the wet cloth to the bathroom after he obviously had cleaned her up. This losing time had to stop.

"Welcome back," he said.

"Did I pass out?"

"You did." Thane smirked at her.

"You are pretty proud of that accomplishment, aren't you?" Angelique raised an eyebrow at him.

Thane gave her a devilish grin. "It's good for my ego. Nothing like giving you so much pleasure you black out from it. Thank you, beautiful, that was amazing, and we both needed the release." Thane lowered himself down onto the bed next to her. "We've had a long day—you especially." He tapped her hip. "Move over. We both need a good night's sleep."

"I've never spent the night with a man before." When his eyes widened, she regretted revealing that secret.

Thane slipped under the sheets and curled up against her. With the gentlest of touches, he stroked her shoulder, her waist, and then her hip. "I'll try to make it a good experience. If I snore, just nudge me, and I'll roll over."

"Oh, I will." Angelique had no idea if she snored. She hoped not.

Facing each other, they leaned forward at the same time and kissed. Maybe she should consider staying here for the next two weeks until the Four Sisters returned. If Thane remained here with her, she'd definitely consider it.

WHEN THANE ROUSED the next morning, his legs were tangled in the sheets, and the most divine blonde had her face on his chest, sleeping soundly. He smiled as he remembered what happened after they returned to the safe house. At first, he'd been more afraid than he ever had in his life. Angelique had been close to death, and there was nothing he could do about it. Once Declan called in a favor and brought in a goddess from Earth, the healing began. As far as he could tell, Angelique was as good as new. Thane still worried though that Mange would come after her, but he would do his best to protect her. If he learned one thing, it was that Mange was not a skilled fighter—or had the dragon he inhabited been the unskilled one? Damn. Uncertainty sucked.

All three of the bodies the dark entity had inhabited had been about the same age, and all three had been males. Whether Mange had a reason for his selection process, Thane had no idea. He just wanted the guy gone.

A hand reached between his legs and grabbed his morning erection. "Someone's up," Angelique said with a smile even though her eyes were closed.

"It's always up when you're near."

Angelique pushed up on an elbow and opened her eyes. "You always say the nicest things."

He leaned down and kissed the top of her head. "Ready for an hour-long flight to the middle of the realm?"

"What do you mean?"

"There is a very special lady I want you to meet. Her name is Fay Forrester. I think she might be able to help us."

"How?" Angelique asked, sounding very interested.

"I can't say exactly, but she has many similarities to you."

She sat up. "Really? Like what?"

"She can turn into points of light, and she has special powers."

"I would like to meet her, but do you think it's wise to leave the safe house?"

Angelique must not be feeling well. "You're usually not this cautious. Why the change?"

"I don't know. I shouldn't be. I shot him with enough white light to disrupt his senses—just like he did mine. Most likely he'll take the day off to recuperate. He won't have a goddess to save him like I did."

"Let's hope that's true. Even if it isn't, I don't plan on hiding from him."

"Then I guess I can't let you out of my sight!"

When the familiar sparkle lit her eyes, he chuckled. "The next time I encounter him, I might have to thank Mange, if it means you'll stay with me all the time."

She shook her head. "Let's hope the next time we run into him, we kill him for good."

"Amen. Ready to see if we can find Fay Forrester?"

"Absolutely."

Thane pulled out his phone. "I'm calling Griffin and Declan to make them aware of our plans."

She tapped his temple. "Good idea. You are always thinking ahead."

He smiled. "I'm glad you think so." After he made the two calls, he patiently listened to his brother and cousin each tell him to be careful. "I'll check in when we return so you can relax. And thank you." He turned to Angelique. "Ready?"

"Yes."

Once he shifted outside, he lifted up Angelique and pointed her downward since she told him that she wanted to watch the landscape pass by from high above the ground.

The trip to the middle of Tarradon should be an easy flight, but only if Thane remained on high alert. No telling what that dark entity would do next. Angelique said she would tap his talon three times if she sensed Mange had taken over another dragon shifter's body.

For once, he wished he could just enjoy the ride with this wonderful woman in his grasp and not have to worry about someone killing them with invisible dark light. What scared Thane the most was that he had no idea how to defend against this monster should it attack.

On the trip over, the wind was minimal, and the sun was out in full, making it a perfect day to fly. When he finally spotted the edge of the forest where Fay resided, he relaxed. He'd been to the eternal flame once before but hadn't seen the fairy there. If it weren't for meeting Fay at Birk and Lily's wedding, he wouldn't have believed she even existed.

Due to the dense foliage, Thane had to land on the outskirts. Once on the ground, he released Angelique.

"That was great, but I'm happy to be on terra firma," she said.

Holding still for an hour would be tiring. "You can stretch your legs on the twenty-minute hike into the woods where the eternal flame is located."

"I've heard mention of it, but I don't really know what it is. Why is this flame so special?"

He explained its origin and how its goal was to unite all of the provinces so they wouldn't battle against each other but rather fight outside invaders.

"Outside invaders?" she asked.

"That's what I've been told. It's possible these invaders were dark entities, or they could have been from another realm, like Cargonia."

She wrapped her arms around her body. "I wouldn't be surprised if the dark entities caused a lot of problems."

He chuckled. "After seeing what Mange can do, neither would I. Come on. Let's see if we can find Fay."

Chapter Ten

EVEN THOUGH ANGELIQUE spent her whole life around light—both white and dark—she was excited to discover the secret of Fay Forrester.

"Is she some kind of psychic?" Angelique asked Thane as they continued down the path. "You said she might know things."

"I don't think she can tell the future, but she kind of sees things."

Angelique had never heard of anyone who was omniscient. "You said she can alter her form at will, from a body into light?"

"It's more like she can disintegrate—if that's the right word—into pricks of light. When Fay came to Lily's wedding, she turned into what looked like a mass of fireflies. When she's not in her light form, she either takes the shape of a six-inch fairy or a rather short woman."

"I'd say we're quite different. Not only can't I see into the future or change into light at will, I'm certainly not a short woman."

Thane wrapped a protective arm around her. "That you are not. I love that you are tall. I don't have to bend down as far to kiss you." As if to prove his point, he leaned over and brushed his lips against hers, and that mere touch made her pulse soar. Stupid libido.

She leaned back. "None of that. We're in the middle of the woods. No telling who might be around here."

"If I believed we'd be undisturbed, I'd be in you now."

She laughed. "You are such a guy."

Thane puffed out his chest. "Would you have me any other way?"

"Absolutely not!"

Hand in hand, they walked down the wide dirt trail. The wind picked up and Angelique stiffened.

"What is it?" he asked. "Is it Mange?"

"No, but I'm sensing someone."

His grip lightened. "I bet it's Fay. I imagine she'll be as interested in meeting you as you are in meeting her."

When they reached the end of the path, it wasn't what she'd pictured. A fountain of sorts with four pipes sticking out of the rock wall sat to the right of a cement bowl that contained what she guessed was the eternal flame.

Thane slipped his hand in his pocket and removed a coin. "We need to make a wish."

"What does a coin have to do with wishing for something?"

"Humor me. Come on. I'll show you." He placed the coin in her hand and had her face the fountain. "Close your eyes and make a wish. Once you're done, open them, and toss the coin in the water."

That seemed like a ridiculous superstition. Then again, she knew little of this realm's ways. "And then what?"

"Hopefully Fay will make an appearance, and your wish will come true."

She skewed her lips to the side. "That seems rather suspicious to me."

He shrugged. "We won't know until you try it."

"Okay, but what am I supposed to wish for?"

He laughed. "I can't tell you. It's for you to decide."

"Fine." Angelique debated between wishing that Thane would fall in love with her, or that Mange would return to his realm without harming anyone else. In the end, she wished that Thane fell in love with her, since that might be the more difficult of the two to achieve.

After making her wish, she opened her eyes and tossed the coin in the fountain.

Leaves rustled behind them, causing her to spin around. In front of her stood a beautiful woman with blonde hair. Considering the glow surrounding this woman, they might have more in common than she first realized. "Hello," Angelique said.

The woman smiled and held out her hand. "I don't think I've had the pleasure of meeting your friend, Thane."

With a hand to her lower back, Thane escorted Angelique closer to the petite blonde. "This is Angelique, my mate."

They shook hands. "You are special, I see," Fay said.

"Like you, I am white light."

Fay suddenly morphed into a tiny creature, and when she fluttered around Angelique and Thane, a sense of warmth filled her. Angelique's heartbeat slowed, almost as if she had been transported to some euphoric state.

A moment later, the small blonde woman stood in front of them once more, but this time she wasn't smiling. "I'm sensing trouble."

That was an understatement. "A dark entity escaped from my realm. I was allowed to leave because Fate asked me to come to Tarradon to watch over the children of the Guardians." She looked up at Thane and took his hand. "And to be with my mate."

"I'm happy for you both, but I sense this dark entity has other plans for you."

Thane squeezed Angelique's hand as a signal for her to tell her tale. "Most likely. Do you know what his plans are?"

"No, I'm sorry."

Angelique explained what Mange had already done and how he'd managed to avoid detection. "When he was attacking me, I managed to pour only some of my light into him. If it hadn't been for the help of a goddess, I might still be unconscious." Or dead.

Fay paced. She eventually stopped and faced both of them.

"There is one way to defeat him," Fay said, her gaze off to the side and her finger pointing. "Yes, I'm sure of it."

Angelique's pulse soared. "What can I do?"

"Mate with Thane. He will inherit your white light and you his magic. Together your powers will be stronger than most in this realm, allowing you to eliminate this scourge permanently."

Thane wrapped an arm around Angelique's waist and squeezed. "Wow, that's amazing and fantastic. Thank you," he said.

"You're very welcome, but you will need to be careful. This Mange is crafty." Fay smiled and then disappeared.

Wait! Damn, Angelique still had questions, the most pressing of which was even if they mated could she take Mange down alone or did the two of them have to be together? Angelique also wanted to ask if she'd ever be able to shift. Even though she'd been told she'd couldn't regardless who she mated with, she wanted a second opinion.

Poor Thane. He'd be so disappointed to learn she couldn't be his mate in the truest sense if she couldn't fly away with him. On the other hand, he would become even more powerful when he mated with her. The white light she would give him could cripple even the worst of the dark lighters.

He turned her around. "What do you think? Once we mate, when we both hit Mange with our white light, we could finally eliminate him," Thane said.

The gold scales on his hands pulsed, and his eyes sparkled. Clearly, this was what he wanted.

Angelique had reservations. "I'm not sure."

"Not sure about what? Whether our combined powers can take him out or about mating with me?" he asked.

You've never told me you loved me. Angelique realized she was being petty since romance had no place in their survival.

"Neither. It's just that we don't know each other all that well. Mating is a huge step, even though I am in complete agreement that Fate sent me here to be with you." She hadn't meant to sound so clinical, but if she allowed emotion to color her decision, she would give in too soon.

A wave of darkness crossed his face. "Really? We don't know each other? After all we've been through?" He cupped her face. "Angelique, I want you. I need you. You are my mate. I thought you felt the same way."

That might be the closest thing to a proclamation of love that she'd get. "I do, but can we go on a date first before we take the plunge?"

Thane lowered his arms. "You want to date when Mange could kill you at any moment?"

He wouldn't kill her—or so she hoped—but he might kill Thane. She didn't want to sound stupid, but she had her reasons. "Just one date, and then we'll mate."

"That's all?"

"Yes."

"A date it is." Thane grinned. "Where would you like to go?"

"Someplace where Mange won't want to be."

"Okay. We can discuss our plans on the way back to the open area." After they walked down the path in silence for a bit, he stopped. "I have a destination in mind. If he tries to get near us, we'll notice him."

"Where's that?"

Thane grinned. "Let me surprise you. As soon as we arrive back in Avonbelle, we'll stop at your place so you can pick up a bathing suit, and then I'll grab mine."

"Our big date is going swimming?"

He frowned. "Don't tell me you never learned how to swim."

She'd never been, but it didn't look too hard. Angelique lifted her chin. "It won't be a problem."

"Good. We aren't actually going swimming. I plan to rent a canoe so we can travel around one of the prettiest lakes in all of Avonbelle Province."

Angelique had to admit she liked this side of Thane. Not only was he romantic, he loved to challenge her to try new things. Yup, the man was a keeper.

THANE MIGHT NOT have thought through this date completely. When they arrived at the lake, the ranger handed them life preservers and paddles, and then showed them to a long wooden dock where a canoe was tied up.

"Just bring her back by six. Don't want you to get lost in the dark," he said with some kind of strange accent.

Since Angelique was looking around with apparent wonder, this man must not have been taken over by Mange. For now, they would be safe.

"We'll be back by then for sure." Thane wasn't about to comment that with his excellent night vision, it would be impossible to lose sight of the shore or this dock. Worst case, he'd figure out a place to shift and then fly them to safety.

Thane held out his hand to her. "Step into the middle of the canoe but be careful because it's not that steady. Face forward and sit on the front seat." Making sure Angelique didn't fall, Thane kept his grip tight. Once she sat down, he stepped in.

"I've never done this before," she said. "Have you?"

"Once. I figured it would be fun for us to learn to do something together."

"I like that idea." Angelique grinned. Yes! He'd chosen wisely. "What do I do with the paddle?" she asked.

"You'll be the one steering. If you put the paddle in the water on the right side of the canoe, we'll go right. And vice versa. Don't worry about trying to move us forward. I'll do the majority of the work."

Once they settled in, Thane pushed off. While the lake was over a hundred acres in size, the calm winds made the water smooth and easy to maneuver on. It took a bit of work to get them in sync, but eventually they were able to make their way along the shore.

They'd been moving for about twenty minutes when Angelique stood up. Before he could remind her how unsteady the canoe was, she lost her balance and fell in.

"Angelique!" He held out his hand. "Take a hold. I'll help you get in." Thank goodness she was wearing her life preserver.

Clearly, he wasn't paying attention because when he bent over to help her, she yanked hard enough to cause him to go head first into the water. When he emerged, Angelique was laughing.

"You did that on purpose?" he asked, not understanding why anyone would do that.

"Of course I did. While the views were lovely, it was hard to talk to you while looking straight ahead."

"Why didn't you say something? We could have stopped and chatted."

With her paddle in hand, she kicked her way over to him. "I felt like a swim."

He'd never known anyone like her before. "But you've never been swimming."

She tapped the life preserver. "This makes it easy."

He tried to stand so he could right the canoe but found he wasn't able to touch bottom. She continued to swim around him, holding onto the paddle for support.

"Help me right this," he said.

"How?"

"Press down on your end while I lift my mine." Within seconds, they had it flipped.

"Ugh, it's full of water," she said.

"We'll have to swim it back to shore and empty it out."

Angelique smiled. "Or we could have some fun in the water first."

He laughed. "Weren't you the one who accused me of having sex on my mind all the time?"

She dipped her chin. "I remember saying no such thing."

"Ah ha. Is that how this is going to be?" he asked.

"What do you mean?" she reached below the water and grabbed his covered cock.

Needing to make sure she was safe before engaging in wild crazy sex in the lake, he lifted her hand from his crotch. "You distract me,

Angelique Carson."

"Good. I'm trying to."

He stilled for a moment. "How do I know Mange didn't take over your body? You're usually not this *friendly*."

Treading water, she grabbed his face and kissed him. When she wrapped her legs around his body and pressed her pussy against his erect cock, Thane totally believed this was Angelique and not some dark monster.

When he hugged her though, the life preserver was in the way. Thane leaned back. "How about we take this to the shore?"

She looked around. "There's a small sandy beach over there we could use."

"With what I have in mind, that's going to be too public."

She pressed her body against his, but their vests made it impossible for him to feel much. More than anything, Thane needed her naked.

"What do you propose?"

"Let's move the canoe to shore, and I'll show you."

Together, they pushed and guided the boat to the sandy beach. Once on solid ground, he lifted it up and dumped out the water. After setting it down, he took off his vest, and Angelique did the same thing.

She smiled. "Much better. I miss seeing your chest."

With her gaze focused on him, she approached, but he held up his hands. "I thought we'd fly out of here and find someplace more secluded. What do you say?"

She stroked her chin. "How about we hike through the woods a bit and find someplace comfortable? It's more adventurous that way. And take your vest. It might come in handy." She winked.

"And here you led me to believe you were full of white light."

"I am," she said acting all innocent.

"I think you are the devil in disguise." He tapped the tip of her nose.

She laughed. "Don't tell me you believe in a real devil?"

"Not exactly, but Mange seems to fit the bill."

Angelique sobered. "You're right about that. Come on. Let's see how much trouble we can get into."

Angelique had always come across as a woman with a wicked business sense, not someone with a wicked sense of humor. She'd only arrived in Edendale a short time ago yet had managed to build a solid business in only a few months. While he'd seen her laugh, he'd never experienced this spicy side of her—and he really liked it.

Too many of his family members complained that all he did was work, claiming his focus was on fighting and defeating evil and not on enjoying himself. Looking at Angelique made him realize what they said might be true. From now on, he would heed their advice. It was time to have some fun. That didn't mean he'd let down his guard for the evil demon threatening to harm them.

Thane followed Angelique into the woods. Except for a few furry sardons racing up and down the trees, no one was about—at least not of the shifter variety. They hiked up a ridge and were able to admire the view of the lake below. Too bad the path on both sides dropped off too steeply to make enjoying this delightful woman possible.

Angelique stopped and pointed. "Is that a cave through those trees?"

"I've never been around here before, but let's check it out. I hope you don't mind spiders, rats, or bats." He wanted to see what she was really made of.

She spun around and punched him. "Are you trying to scare me? I'll make sure even the scariest animals stay away from us."

He laughed. "You are such a joy."

"Is that so? Then come on and show me how much."

When they stepped inside, darkness enveloped them. While his shifter vision allowed him to see just fine, he took Angelique's hand. "Better let me lead."

Even though they both had a sexual encounter in mind, this was a date, and he wanted her to have a great experience. Thane needed to show Angelique how much she meant to him, that he—the man—desired her just as much if not more than his horny dragon. The last thing he needed was a woman who mated with him because it was the only way to keep them both safe.

Thane took a right turn down a cave tunnel and halted. Angelique bumped into him.

"What is it?" she asked.

Thane moved to the side to let her see the incredible view. Before them was a grotto of sorts with a large clear pool of aquamarine blue water that seemed to be lit from below.

"It's amazing," Angelique said. "I've never seen anything like it before."

He hadn't either. "Let me see if it's safe to swim in."

"Why wouldn't it be?"

"Oh, I don't know. Maybe Mange managed to lure us here somehow and poisoned the water before we arrived." Okay, that sounded really paranoid, and Thane was not the conspiracy theory type, but he didn't want to rule it out.

She placed a hand on his. "That's not how he works. When, or rather if, Mange comes after me, he'll harm me with his darkness, not hurt me with some poison. How about we enjoy this beautiful adventure and not let that evil being spoil our date?"

Angelique was a truly remarkable woman. "You read my mind."

Before he could stop her, Angelique jumped in without her life preserver. Wanting to make sure she stayed safe, he went in after her and found the water temperature significantly warmer than the lake. Nice. It was almost as if a hot spring fed this grotto.

Angelique surfaced and moved toward him, sometimes kicking her legs and other times propelling herself with her arms. While he wouldn't really call it swimming, she was trying.

Once Angelique was close enough, she reached out and wrapped herself around him. "This is incredible. Had you heard of this place before?" she asked.

"Nope. This is new for both of us."

"It's cozy in here," she said in between kisses. "And very private."

"It is. You don't sense anyone closing in on us, do you?"

She blew out a breath. "If I did, I'd tell you. Now can we get back to what I want to do?"

Thane floated on his back and dragged Angelique on top of him, her back to his chest. "Let's float here for a bit and enjoy nature." His little minx wiggled her butt, setting off his internal need.

"You're no fun," she said as she reached between her legs and tried to grab hold of his dick.

That was it. With two powerful kicks, Thane reached the edge of the grotto. He swung her off him and moved her onto the rocky ledge. "Stay there."

A second later he was on the solid ground that was composed of intermittent rocks and sand. He lifted her up and set her on a sandy part.

"You are strong," she said with lust in her eyes.

"Strip," he commanded.

She grinned "Yes, sir."

In seconds, Angelique took off her two-piece black bathing suit while he stepped out of his trunks. Now to do what he'd wanted since this date started.

Chapter Eleven

A NGELIQUE HAD NO idea that Thane could be so spontaneous. She looked around their private retreat for a place to enjoy him. Aw hell. Even though it was mostly rocks, that wouldn't deter her. She picked up her life preserver, dropped it on the uneven ground and knelt down in front of him. As quick as she could, she reached for his cock with one hand while she drew his butt closer with her other.

"To think I thought you were almost angelic," Thane said with a sparkle in his teal eyes.

"Even as a pure white entity, there has always been a bit of bad girl in me just waiting to get out. Actually, it was when I met you that I finally let that side have some sinful pleasures."

Thane laughed. "You are good for my soul, Angelique." When she drew him deep into her mouth, he sucked in an audible breath. "And for my needs," he whispered.

They'd just made love last night, so why did she crave him so quickly and intensely? Fate sure was working its magic on her. Thane grabbed a handful of her wet hair and twirled it around his fist. Given all of his grunts, he was enjoying this interlude as much as she was. Pumping her fist hard, she licked the side of his cock before encompassing it again. She yearned to have Thane touch her in this intimate way too.

"Your turn." He practically shouted his demand as he lifted her to her feet. "Wait here."

He nabbed his life preserver, placed it above hers, and then slowly lowered her onto her back. He knelt and spread her legs. Oh my, yes. This was exactly what she hoped they'd be doing today.

He leaned over and drew her tit into his mouth, sending sparks of desire straight through her. She clawed at his shoulders and then dragged her palms down his muscled biceps. Thane might be slick with water, but his pheromones were filling the space with a delicious scent. In theory, shifters had more intense reactions to everything, but she bet white entities had just as much.

He pinched her nipple with one hand as he slid his fingers between her legs, delving them into her opening. Angelique bucked. "Please take me now."

Thane slid his hand from her breast to her cheek and then kissed her. The combination of their tongues tangling and his finger relentlessly pressing on her most sensitive spot caused her climax to nearly swallow her whole. Even she was surprised at the brightness and intensity of her white light and how it nearly encircled them both.

Thane removed his finger and was about to mount her when he stopped and looked toward the exit.

Oh, shit. Was Mange coming? Had she been so involved in Thane that she hadn't sensed him? "What is it?"

"I'm sensing two Guardians."

She relaxed. "Guardians are good. Maybe they're on some secret mission."

The tension in his shoulders seemed to relax. "You're right. That must be it. Now where were we?"

Angelique smiled and then reached between them to grab his cock. "I think you can figure out what comes next."

Thane's body lit up gold, and it was the most beautiful sight in the world. The grotto water shimmered off the walls, making his eyes more leafy green than teal.

As Thane's tongue plunged into her mouth, he spread her legs wider with his knees, and then drove into her. Euphoria swamped her. It was almost as if she'd been put into her body for this precise reason. They wouldn't mate tonight, but they would soon. Very soon.

When he retreated and plowed in again, all thoughts of the future disappeared and were replaced by the total bliss prickling her skin. Erotic lust encased her as her glow increased.

Wanting it harder and faster, she pressed the soles of her feet onto the life preserver and lifted her butt. Her hands roamed all over his body, unable to fully satisfy her needs. With each stroke, her second orgasm brimmed.

"I can't get enough of you," Thane panted.

His words held such passion that Angelique could no longer hold back. On the next thrust, she came. With her eyes closed, she let the glory infuse every cell of her being.

Thane lowered his hands to her waist and hammered into her once more. A second later, his seed exploded, and they became one. Her joy was so great, a small tear leaked out of her eye. It was at that moment that she realized how much she loved Thane Sinclair.

He slipped out of her, stood, and held out his hand. When she reached out for it, he helped her to her feet. Thane carefully led her the few feet to the water.

"One more quick rinse before we head back. We don't want to piss off the canoe ranger and arrive after dark," he said.

She laughed. "Totally."

After they thoroughly cleaned—and kissed many more times— he helped her out of the warm grotto water. They both dressed in relative silence and headed out the way they came.

As soon as they exited the cave, Thane stopped and looked up.

"What is it?" she asked. Angelique had never seen Thane this intense.

"Griffin and Declan are circling up above. Something's up."

"You told them we were coming here. Maybe they just want to make sure Mange didn't get us. After all, we ditched the canoe in plain sight."

"Could be, but it's not like them. Let's hoof it back. I'd fly us, but the foliage is pretty dense, and I don't think you'd appreciate being scraped up."

"I don't mind if it's for a good cause."

He reached out and dragged a knuckle down her cheek. "I'm sure they can wait a little longer."

Once they reached the river, Griffin and Declan were waiting for them.

"We've been screeching for half an hour. Didn't you hear us?" Declan asked, sounding a bit agitated.

"Yes, but I thought you might be passing by on a mission," Thane said.

"No. Something happened. And it isn't good."

Thane stiffened. "What is it?"

Griffin glanced over at Angelique and stepped closer to her. "I'm sorry to tell you that there was a fire at your coffee shop."

Her knees nearly buckled. Thane slipped a hand around her waist that kept her from crashing to the ground. "A fire? How bad was it? Was anyone hurt?"

"No one was hurt. Melissa rushed everyone out in time, but there's quite a lot of smoke damage."

Angelique sucked in a deep breath. "Do you know the cause of the fire?"

Griffin shook his head. "I'm sorry. Josh Gerrard, the arson investigator, is on the case. I imagine he'll know more when you get there."

She looked up at Thane. "I'd like to go now."

Declan stepped over to the canoe. "You three take off. I'll return the canoe and the gear. Then I'll catch up."

"Thanks," Thane said. He faced her. "We'll head back to your place to change. Then we can go to the coffee shop."

"Yes, that sounds good. Thank you."

The trip back was wrought with worry. Angelique hoped the fire was just an accident in the kitchen and not that Mange had set it. If only she knew whether he was trying to drive her back to her realm or if he was threatened by her assignment, she might be able to figure things out. Sure, his goal in life was to cause disruption, but why target her?

After a rather grueling flight, they landed on her front lawn.

"Do you sense him anywhere?" Thane asked.

She inhaled and then closed her eyes to calm her anger. Angelique needed all of her senses alert. No telling what that ass was capable of. She let out her breath. "No."

He held out his palm for the key. While she was quite capable of letting herself in, Angelique understood Thane's need to be in charge—and his need to protect her. She unhooked the key that she'd attached to her bathing suit bottom and handed it to him.

Once inside, he insisted on looking in every room first before he allowed her to walk about freely.

"All clear. Why don't you pack for a few days," Thane said.

"Sure." It didn't take her long to throw her clothes in a bag. "I'm ready," she said as she returned to the living room.

Thane slipped the case from her fingers. "Let's take your car so we can move about the city easier."

After they stopped off at his place for Thane to change, they drove into town. Fire trucks lined the streets in front of her shop, and her stomach spun. "The front looks undamaged at least."

"That's a good thing. Hey, there's Josh. He should have some answers by now."

As soon as they approached, Josh ended his conversation with someone and came over to them. "Ms. Carson. I tried to reach you before."

"Thane and I were out of town. How bad is it?"

"The kitchen sustained some damage, but you were lucky. Someone put out the fire almost before it began."

She looked up at Thane and then back at Josh. "I don't understand."

"I don't either. According to one eyewitness, some dragon shifter was flying overhead. He must have smelled the smoke, because one minute he seemed to be minding his business, and the next he'd torn a hole in the roof and shot enough water into the kitchen to put out the fire."

That sounded preposterous, but she wasn't from this world, so maybe there were such things as water dragons.

Thane nodded. "Do we know who this mysterious dragon is?"

"No, but he made our job easier. We're working to drain the inside of water now. Thankfully, the damage was contained to your shop."

That was good luck. "Tarradon is full of heroes," she said.

"So it appears," Josh said.

"Could you tell how the fire started?" Thane asked.

"I'm working on it. My preliminary guess is arson."

"What about Donald? Was he in the kitchen at the time?" Angelique asked.

"He was knocked out cold. That is one reason why I'm saying it was arson."

Thane slipped her hands into his. "Let us know if you find out anything more. Can we go inside?"

"Not for a few more hours. Not only isn't it safe to breathe the air, the floors are still slippery. I'll call you when you can return and begin cleaning up."

"Thank you," she said.

As Thane escorted her back to the car, she briefly sensed evil nearby, but by the time she thought she identified the location, it was gone. Angelique should probably mention it to Thane, but he'd insist on locking her up in the safe house while he left to investigate, which would be the worst thing he could do. She wished she knew how to convince him that no amount of dragon power could defeat someone—or rather something—as evil as Mange.

Griffin was waiting for them back at the car. "How bad is it?" he asked.

Angelique gave him the rundown. "It would have been a lot worse if it hadn't been for some water dragon."

"That's the second time he saved someone or something that we know of," Griffin said. "My sister Nessa was the first to run into him. He saved her and her mate."

"Wow. I'm guessing that dragons don't usually go around spewing water?"

"No. He's the only one I've heard of."

That gave her pause. "He must not be from around here then."

"I doubt he came from here originally. He might even be from another realm."

She wanted to meet this water dragon to see if he was some white entity who helped others in a different way.

Griffin faced both of them. "I'm going to hang out here for the night. I'm sure there will be other security, but I want to be here just in case."

"Why?" she asked.

"I wouldn't put it past this ass to return to see the havoc he caused."

Her heart squeezed tight at that terrible thought. "That is so nice of you, but if it is Mange, he will be dangerous."

"I'll be careful."

Thane placed a hand on his cousin's shoulder. "Ask Stone to take over for you if you need a break. We should have someone here twenty-four-seven, or at least until Angelique is up and running again."

That made her feel so indebted. "You don't have to do that. I can hire a firm to watch my place. Thane, you and your family have done so much for me already." The problem was that she doubted the cops had the manpower to be here all day.

"Griffin's right. Our family needs to be in charge." Thane said. "I don't trust Mange not to take over one of the bodies of someone hired by the security firm."

Shit. That was an even scarier thought. "Who says he can't take over yours or Griffin's body just as easily?"

He lifted an eyebrow. "Because we're Guardians."

"That didn't mean he can't. You aren't invincible."

"We're at least aware of what he can do. I'm hoping we have the skills to fight him off."

She wasn't going to argue with him, but even she alone didn't have the power.

After saying goodbye to Griffin, and thanking him once more, they piled into her car. Instead of heading back to the mines, Thane stopped at the police station.

"What are we doing here?" she asked.

He shut off the engine and faced her. "I want to see if Anderson has found any more dead bodies."

"Mange has no reason to change bodies unless he suspects someone saw him light the fire—assuming he is the arsonist."

"I agree. Do you have security cameras at the coffee shop?"

"In the main area, sure, but not in the kitchen. Even if Mange entered the shop, he could have taken over any of the people in there. I'm betting he's learning how to fool the family and friends of this person into believing he hasn't changed. No one would even report their loved one missing in that case."

Just saying those words scared her.

"Good point. Where do you keep the copy of the surveillance footage?"

She smiled. "In the cloud. No one can access it except for me or my two assistants." Reality dawned. "Crap. I'm calling Melissa and Shannon to see if anyone approached them about accessing the files. He could have had a timer to set the charge and then pretend to be from the security company. He'd want to erase the feed or tamper with it somehow so he couldn't be identified."

"That is a scary thought." Thane pushed open his car door. "Let's bring Anderson up to speed and see what he suggests."

Once inside, they asked to speak with him in private.

"Let's head on into one of the offices. They're nicer than the interrogation room."

"Thank you. Do you know anything more about the fire?" she asked.

"Nothing more than the arson investigator told me."

Once they were seated in the office, Thane told them about his theory that Mange might have been involved. Angelique pulled out her computer that she'd picked up from home and accessed the video of her shop. "Nothing looks out of place right before the fire. Just customers ordering and such."

"Did anyone approach Melissa or Shannon?" Thane asked.

"The camera isn't aimed at the offices." Once she opened the shop again, she'd change that.

Angelique watched a bit longer and then stilled. "Oh, no. I think we have a problem."

"What is it?" Anderson asked.

Chapter Twelve

"SOMEONE TAMPERED WITH the feed," Angelique said, as she twisted around her screen. "See the woman with the red shirt and short brown hair?"

"Yes," Thane said. "What about her?"

"Keep watching. She comes up again a minute later. At first, I thought she was placing a second order, but then Jamie Sanders—the girl in the yellow shirt—walks up next to her as does some man whose back is to us. Those same two people ordered again and stood in the exact same spot."

"Are you saying someone created a loop?" Anderson asked.

"It appears so. Mange must have known about the cameras and then chose the right person to inhabit."

"Are you implying that if Mange takes over someone who is gifted technologically that he would have those skills once he enters them?"

"That appears to be the case."

"Damn it." This complicated things.

Anderson leaned forward on his elbows. "Do you have any idea how to find Mange now?"

She shook her head. "He always finds me. Personally, I don't want to run into him again, especially considering what happened the last time. I just want him to disappear, but clearly, he wants something from me."

"He needs to be stopped." Thane placed a hand on hers. "I'm going to insist you not leave my side, and if I can't be with you, I'll ask someone else to stand watch. Are you okay with that?"

"If it means I can supervise my business and get it up and running again, you can put twenty armed guards on me. Just make sure everyone is aware of what we're dealing with. Mange isn't like an ordinary dark lighter that just does spells. I need to be the one to deal with him—not them."

"I'll make that perfectly clear."

Someone knocked on the office door and poked his head in. "Anderson, sorry to interrupt, but I thought you'd want to know that we found another body like the ones before."

Thane fisted his hand. "Are you saying this person has a burn pattern on his body?"

"Yes."

Anderson pushed back his chair. "Rest assured, we will find him. This Mange fellow will pay."

"He'll pay all right, if it's the last thing I do," Thane said.

The big question was how many more would die before he and Angelique could kill him for good? As much as he wanted to wait a bit longer before they mated, things were heating up too fast for that luxury.

Angelique's jaw had clenched, and he could only guess what she was going through. She probably believed this was all her fault somehow.

He turned toward her. "How long did it take you to go from your realm to ours?" It might be as quick as the portal jump between here and Earth—which was almost instant—or it could take days.

"One second. Why?"

Shit. "I was just trying to figure out if Mange exited your realm with you, or if he came at a different time."

"The more I think about it, the more convinced I am that Fate let him out. I believe I would have sensed him if he'd come with me, despite the short duration of the trip."

As long as he lived, Thane might never understand the universe and its mysterious ways. He stood and then took her hand as she got up as well. "Let's go back to the safe house and forget about all of this for one night—if we can," he said.

Her smile came out weak. "I'd like that, but I'll need something to distract me." Angelique planted a hand on his chest.

That made him smile. "You're speaking my language."

They were halfway back to the safe house when her cell rang. Angelique checked the screen. "It's Melissa."

"Good. Maybe she can fill you in with what really happened."

"Melissa, how are you?" Angelique said with a lot of concern in her voice. "I'm putting you on speaker so Thane can hear too."

"I'm fine. Shannon is here with me also. We're both good physically. Mentally, we're still shaken."

"I can only imagine. Tell me what happened."

"It was terrifying. All I can say is thank goodness for that dragon shifter who put out the fire. People were yelling, smoke was pouring out of the kitchen, and…"

"Whoa. What? Slow down, and start from the beginning."

"Okay, okay. When the fire started, I was in the office," Melissa said.

"And I was working the cash register," Shannon chimed in.

"Did you see anyone suspicious, like someone heading to the kitchen around the time of the blaze?" Angelique asked. "I know the bathrooms are down the hallway, but something might have seemed off."

"No. I had no idea anything was wrong until I heard a commotion in the kitchen. It sounded like pots crashing," Shannon said. "When I went to check it out, I found Donald on the floor out cold with a spatula still in his hand. His lip was split as if someone had punched him. Just as I bent down to see if I could help, I smelled the smoke. It wasn't long before I realized the stove was on fire."

"Did you try to put it out?" Angelique asked.

"Yes, but the fire extinguisher wasn't where it normally is."

Angelique looked over at Thane. He failed to unclench his jaw or release his tight grip on the wheel. He wanted to destroy Mange worse than anything.

"I checked the extinguisher the other day," Angelique said.

"I know you did. The arsonist must have done something with it. I was about to call for help when I was hit on the head."

Angelique nearly dropped her cell. "Oh, my goddess. You said you were all right."

"I am now."

"Oh, Shannon. I'm so sorry."

"Thank you. I have a headache, but the cut on my scalp didn't require stitches. I was lucky."

"I walked in on her right after it happened," Melissa cut in. "The backdoor slammed shut, but I wasn't about to run outside to see who it was—not with two people on the floor and the kitchen on fire. I helped Shannon up, and after we checked that the alley was clear, we dragged Donald outside. Even then the smoke was quite intense. I rushed inside and grabbed the money and receipts and called for help. Then I ushered everyone out."

"That was so smart of you. I really appreciate it."

"Thank you."

"What about Donald?"

"I went out the front like everyone else and then rushed around to the back where we'd put Donald. By then, he'd come to."

"When did this water dragon show up?" Angelique asked.

"Right after that. The fire engines were coming down the street. That's when I looked up and spotted this big, blue dragon clawing a hole in the roof and then dumping a ton of water inside the coffee shop. Apparently, that did the trick."

She still couldn't wrap her head around all of it. "Then what?"

"I returned to the front to find help. The paramedics were there. They headed to the back with me to check out Shannon and Donald," Melissa said.

"How is Donald?"

Thane held his breath. This was a nightmare.

"He's in the hospital now. The paramedics said he had a concussion and they want to check him out. I wouldn't be surprised if he needs some stitches too."

"Thanks for letting me know." Angelique glanced over at Thane, her lips pressed together. "You two get some rest, and we'll talk tomorrow," she said.

"I'm sorry about the shop, Angelique."

"It'll be back up and running before you know it. And don't worry about your jobs. Everyone will remain on the payroll." She swiped the off button and rested her head back.

Angelique was an amazing woman. Her entire business had almost been demolished and yet she'd kept her cool. She'd make a great addition to not only the Guardian organization but to his life.

The Sinclair Mine came into view, and Thane pulled down the entrance road. "Be right back," he said.

At the wall, he retrieved a scale from his pocket, swiped it across the stone until the spot glowed and the garage door appeared. As it opened up fully, he jogged back to the car and drove into an undesignated space. "Ready to have a relaxing evening?"

She actually smiled. "I'm more than ready."

Thane was starving. First, he'd satisfy his stomach and then he'd satisfy his more prurient urges. "Let's see what's in the kitchen. The cook will be gone for the night, but I bet we can whip up something."

"You cook?"

Thane laughed. Now that they were safe, he could let down his guard. He was so ready to enjoy himself. Even though his body still was thrumming from their lovemaking earlier today, he wanted more. Much more. "Not really. You?"

"No. Why do you think I decided to open a coffee shop that made sandwiches, pastries, and light snacks? It's not like I had a mother to teach me any culinary skills."

The reality of who she was and how Angelique had been raised hit him hard. Her life growing up had to have been so different. The fact she ended up the way she did, amazed him even more.

He wrapped his arms around her. "I'm sorry. That must have

been tough."

She leaned back and looked up at him. "Not really. I had role models. We might not have possessed bodies, but our minds were able to join as one. We had love, a lot of caring, and many wonderful times." Angelique shrugged. "At least when the dark entities didn't decide they wanted some fun at our expense."

Thane stroked her face. "It seems we learned some of the same lessons about life."

"We did."

Stop the chitchat and take her to bed already, his dragon begged.

I will shortly, but right now I'm hungry. Besides, a grumbling stomach is not sexy.

Fine, but eat fast.

Thane almost laughed at his horny dragon, but more importantly, he wanted to show Angelique that he was able to control his urges—at least sometimes.

"How about I check the fridge while you look in the cabinets. Let me know if anything looks good," Thane said.

"You got it." She scrounged around a bit before pulling out a box. "How about I make some brownies?"

"Works for me, but we need something more nutritious for dinner." He checked the fridge contents. "It looks as if the cook hasn't been in today," he said. "There aren't any leftovers."

"We could order in."

"I had considered that option, but it would be too easy for Mange to sneak in here."

She set down the brownie mix. "Way to spoil my appetite."

Thane gathered her in his arms. "I hope your appetite has only disappeared for food."

Angelique lightly punched him. "You do only think of sex."

Thane tried to show indignation, but he was sure he failed. "Let me show you that's not totally true. I can whip us up some bacon and eggs." When she dragged a hand down his chest and didn't seem to be stopping, he clasped her wrist. "Food first."

"Fine. What can I do?"

"Can you make toast for us?"

Angelique tilted her head. "Now you're being insulting."

Thane swatted her butt and grinned. "Get to it then."

Once she located the loaf of bread, Angelique put four pieces in the toaster and depressed the lever. "If you tell me what to do, I can make the bacon."

"There's a package in the bottom drawer of the fridge. Just place it in a frying pan, turn it to medium heat, and flip when needed."

"Sounds simple enough."

With Angelique taking care of two of the three parts of the meal, all he had to do was crack open a few eggs, add some milk, and beat them.

As they worked together at the stove, a sense of warmth filled him. This companionship had been the missing link in his life. "Working side by side with you is really nice," Thane said.

She smiled. "I like it too."

After blending the eggs, he poured the mixture into the hot pan. As he stirred them, he smelled something burning. Glancing over at the toaster, he exhaled at the billowing smoke. "Ah, Angelique? The toast."

"Oh shit." She ran over and lifted up the toaster lever. "I thought it would come up by itself."

"It usually does. It doesn't matter. We have eggs and bacon." Though the bacon looked burned to a crisp, Thane turned off both burners and then located two plates.

They served themselves and then sat at the table, downing the meal in minutes. "I guess I was hungrier than I thought," Angelique said.

"Me too." He was glad she was able to push aside the tragedy of her shop enough to eat. "Ready to make the brownies?"

"I'm always ready for dessert."

He chuckled. He grabbed the egg while Angelique located the oil, bowl, and wooden mixing spoon. After setting the oven to the right temperature, he poured in the mix, eggs, and water. She added in the oil.

"How about you blend while I find the pan?" he asked.

"You got it," she said.

Thane located the pan and handed it to her. Thane then emptied the contents into it. Just as he was about to place the dish in the oven, she stuck her finger in the mix, scooped up some of the raw batter, and then slowly licked her finger. Thane had controlled his urges all through dinner, but this was too much.

"Is that how you want this night to end?" he asked as he followed suit, but instead of licking the batter, he dabbed a bit on her nose.

Angelique's mouth opened. "You aren't playing fair." Never taking her gaze off him, she lifted off her shirt and sports bra at the same time.

Thane couldn't keep from staring. When she scraped the goo off her nose and smeared it on one tit, his cock hardened to the point of almost bursting. "You're playing with fire, young lady."

She laughed. "Is that a dragon pun—playing with fire?"

It took him a moment to realize what he'd said. "I don't need any of my shifter abilities to heat you up." Thane leaned over and sucked on her deliciously chocolate covered nipple. Not only was the taste divine, being this close to Angelique made him yearn for more.

"Aren't you the cocky one," she said.

Thane chuckled, loving the repartee. Angelique tugged on his shorts.

"Someone's in a hurry," he said.

"I am." With a hard yank, his shorts landed on the floor. He stepped out of them and kicked them aside. While he wasn't positive, he believed they were the only two people in the safe house, but that wasn't to say someone couldn't walk in.

He was about to suggest they take this next stage to the bedroom when she used two fingers to gather more brownie mix. Quicker than he could blink, she slathered the batter on his cock. "Whoops," she said with absolutely no remorse.

"Now look what you've done," he said as gruffly as he could muster. He set down the pan of batter. "Lick it off."

Angelique dropped back her head and laughed. "As if you have to tell me to."

Chapter Thirteen

ANGELIQUE MOTIONED FOR Thane to hop up onto the counter, giving her easy access to him.

"The oven. Crap," she said as she rushed over to turn it off. Baking brownies no longer seemed to be her goal.

Maybe it was because he knew he was about to mate with her that it seemed as if each lick held more promise than ever before. Thane still couldn't believe he'd been chosen by Fate to be her mate. Angelique was not only beautiful, she was courageous, smart, and sexy as hell.

Once she finished lapping up the mess she'd made, Angelique stepped back, kicked off her shoes, and stripped the rest of the way.

"Holy fuck, you are hot." No doubt his eyes were flashing teal.

Not losing eye contact, Thane slipped off the counter. In one step, he had one arm wrapped around her waist and the other under her butt. In one quick move, he lifted her up.

Angelique smiled. "This is going to be a sweet ride."

"Hang on tight, my woman of the light."

She wrapped her arms around his neck and kissed him hard. Their breaths mingled and their exploration turned intense. It was as if they were both hanging on by a thread. How his need was this intense, he didn't understand. When they finally mated, he wasn't sure how he'd handle his desperate desire for her.

Thane walked toward the kitchen door, kicked it closed, and pressed her against it. He lowered his hands to support her rear.

Angelique broke the kiss and leaned back. She glanced down at her tits and then back up at him. "They're all yours."

Thane groaned. "Such a beautiful present."

With that, he leaned over and drew her nipple into his mouth, loving the way the delicate tip swelled under his touch. His cock pressed against her opening, and as much as he wanted to plunge into her right now, he wanted their lovemaking to last.

She lifted her hand from around his neck, grabbed the back of his head, and squeezed. "I'm no longer going to hide how much I need you. Bite me and make me yours."

His animal almost shifted from her acceptance. The kiss that followed was intense. Deep. Passionate. Dynamic.

Mate, mate, his dragon urged as he clawed up a storm, poking the talons out of Thane's fingers and setting his body on fire.

"What are you waiting for?" Angelique panted, her eyes partially glazed over with lust.

"I'm trying to calm down. I want this night to be special. We only get to mate for the first time once in a lifetime."

She smiled. "Such the romantic. Who knew?"

"Only with you. Trust me."

Using the door to help support Angelique, Thane slipped his cock straight into her, lighting him up like never before. They may not have mated yet, but it seemed as if her white light was entering his body.

"You are very slick and oh so divine," he said.

"The easier to fuck you."

He grinned. "Did they teach you to talk like that in your realm?"

Angelique laughed. "You'd be surprised what I know."

"Enough talking and more kissing."

Angelique pressed her breasts against his chest and nibbled her way from his chin up to his eyes. When she returned to his lips, every inch of his body exploded. Thane slid his hands to her waist, holding on tight, as he stroked her harder and harder until his teeth sharpened.

"You're mine now, Angelique."

She dropped her head back and panted, "Yes!"

He lowered his mouth to her delicate neck and pressed his teeth against her skin. She clawed his shoulders and pumped her body up and down. When her mouth opened and her eyes fluttered, he sunk his teeth into her neck, uniting them from now until eternity.

Her white light glowed and encased them both. Heat filled him. Total bliss speared him, and the look in Angelique's eyes convinced him this had been the right moment to mate.

When she tightened her pussy walls and screamed out her release, his cock detonated. Waves of power surged through him as he fully embraced all of what she had to offer. For a brief moment, he thought he'd been transported to her realm. So much light was interspersed with random bits of dark. While Thane couldn't understand all of it, the connection was so intense he nearly burst from a surge of happiness, joy, and dare he say love?

Not wanting to ruin anything by saying those words, he kept quiet.

Once his fangs retracted, he licked her wound and gently kissed her. "You are amazing, my beautiful Angel," he said.

"I can't even find the words to express what I'm feeling."

Still inside her, he walked her to the kitchen counter and set her down before slipping out of her. Using a towel from the drawer, Thane cleaned her up.

Angelique leaned back on her elbows. "I don't know about you, but I think a shower is in order."

Thane grinned. "I couldn't agree more."

"WE'VE BEEN AT this for hours," Angelique said, trying not to whine, but failing miserably. She and Thane were in his studio where he was teaching her the fine art of hand-to-hand combat. Angelique had never worked this hard in her life.

Thane laughed. "You're the one who wants to have her freedom."

"Freedom is about being at my store, not learning to fight." She sounded like a wuss.

"I know you are incredibly powerful and can weaken Mange on your own, but what if Mange comes to your store and manages to get the drop on you again? He could attack you from behind and strangle you. Once you weaken from the lack of oxygen, he could then shoot his dark light into you before you had the chance to shoot your light at him."

"It's possible, but not likely." She held up a hand. "Just so you know, it's not like he can take over my body. That is the one benefit of being a white entity. Don't get me wrong. I want to learn to fight. It might not always be someone from my realm attacking me."

"I agree. Tell me what you'll do if someone comes at you from behind?"

Angelique inhaled. "I'll quickly turn around, bend my knees, and attack him at his waist. I'll punch until I hurt him."

Thane smiled. "Good. Let's try it."

"Why? I just told you what I'd do."

He dipped his chin. "Angelique, please."

She held up her palms in defeat. "Fine."

"You need to understand that if Mange manages to get the drop on you like he did before, I want you to have the time to shoot him with your light."

"I'll be the first to admit this is a good plan, but remember Mange never touched me the last time."

"Could that be because he didn't have a body at the time?" Thane asked.

"Good point." It really gave her confidence that her mate was so well versed in the art of fighting. Now that he had his own well of white light, he too could cripple Mange—or so she wanted to believe.

"Let's do this again," he commanded.

Angelique turned her back to him and tensed. Thane's arm wrapped around her neck, and her instincts kicked in. While not born a fighter, when they had mated, she must have inherited some of his power. All at once, she twisted her head, dropped down, and spun around, nearly toppling both of them. Even though he weighed a lot, she managed to face him.

A second later, she was in his arms and then his lips were on hers. All thoughts of fighting left her as he ran his hands up and down her back. She held onto him tight, pouring her love back into him.

While she was enjoying the break, he swept his leg behind hers, making her lose her balance. He let go and down she went onto the mat.

Thane grinned. "That will remind you not to lose focus."

"That is so not fair. I would never let Mange kiss me."

"I hope not!" Thane grinned and then shrugged. "Just saying that when we are in here, it's all business." Angelique thought she caught him wink, but her hair was hanging over her face, and she couldn't be sure.

Angelique sat up and slipped off her top. As she started to re-move her sports bra, Thane straddled her legs. "What are you doing?" he asked, peering down at her.

He seemed to be fighting a smile. In one quick movement, she lowered her arms and grabbed his leg, hoping to make him lose his balance. The damn beast of a man didn't even move. "I wanted to sidetrack you into losing focus."

He laughed. "Trust me, Angelique, I have a hard time focusing on anything when you are near me."

"Then show some respect and fall over."

A bit upset that her plan failed, she stood and faced him. Thane placed his hands on her shoulders. Because it was like one of the moves he'd taught her, she drove her arms upward with her palms pressed together, and then smashed her elbows into the crook of his arms. This time, she broke his hold.

Her victory was short lived however. Thane dipped his shoulder, pressed it into her midsection, and lifted her. Angelique tensed, knowing what came next. Instead of the slam she expected, he slid her down in front of him and kissed her again.

Truce? she telepathed, thrilled that one of her old skills from back in the realm would be useful again. Being mates had many advantages.

After a long, heady kiss, Thane leaned back. *"Are you saying you want to stop for today?"*

"You'll let me?"

He dragged a knuckle down her cheek. *"I only want to push you as far as you are willing to go. Until Mange is killed, I will have to drive you hard."*

She grinned. *"Or drive hard into me."*

His gold scales flashed. "No talking sexy when your life is in danger."

She stuck out her tongue. "This whole time my life has been in danger, and yet you talk about sex."

"That was before. Not only do I want you ready to take down any man that Mange has inhabited, I want your stamina to be at its peak performance too."

She had to agree that if she'd been in better shape, she might have resisted Mange's darkness long enough to send more of her light into him longer and harder.

"I do too. I guess that means we're moving on to boxing? At least the punching bag won't attack from behind."

He chuckled. "You'd be surprised by the number of injuries caused by that leather beast."

For the next hour, Angelique punched, kicked, and swore at the bag. When her legs wobbled, Thane must have taken pity on her.

"That's all for today," he said. "Let's head back and shower."

Images of them naked raced into her mind. "Sounds awesome, but note I'm lucky if I have enough energy to hold a bar of soap."

Thane leaned in close enough to kiss her. "I can wash you if you want."

She lightly punched him. "I'm too tired for sex—at least I am until after I've eaten."

"Grab your stuff. I have a plan."

After they turned off the lights of his studio and locked up, Thane flew them back to the safe house. He said it was safer to be in the sky than in a car where some maniac might try to harm them. Angelique didn't argue. She wouldn't put anything past the dark entity.

Once they stepped into the bedroom, Thane faced her. "What do you say we go out?"

"I love it, but first let me get clean—by myself. I don't want to be tempted."

"Really? You're not tempted when you're by yourself?"

"Not as much as when I'm near you."

Thane huffed. "Sometimes, I think it's worse when I'm not with you. You consume my every thought."

Aw. She smiled. "You say the sweetest things."

Even though Angelique was sweaty, and Thane smelled none too great, she stood on her tiptoes and kissed his cheek. "I'll hurry."

Tonight was going to be wonderful. Now that they'd mated, and Angelique was a more proficient fighter than before, the threat from Mange to them wasn't as great. Once that ass was sent back to the dark realm—or destroyed completely—they could move on with their lives. Thane was exciting, romantic, and wonderfully unpredictable.

Needless to say, after they returned from their evening out, she had every intention of satisfying her constant need for him.

Chapter Fourteen

"**B**OWLING? SERIOUSLY?" ANGELIQUE asked.

Thane escorted her to her car. "Why not? I've only been bowling once, and you said you've never been, so I figured this will be the perfect new adventure."

Angelique had to laugh. "You're right about that, but as I've said, since we've already done the deed, so to speak, you don't have to feel obligated to take me out again."

"Are you kidding me? We'll be spending the rest of our lives together. I can't wait to learn as much about you as possible. Besides, with all the shit that has happened, I figured we've earned a fun night out."

Thane was so thoughtful. "It will be nice when we can let down our guard," she said.

They hopped into Angelique's car, and Thane drove them to the bowling alley located on the edge of town. "I checked online. Apparently it's league night at Pinarama," Thane said. "Which gives me hope that Mange won't be coming here, though there are a few lanes they keep open for walk-ins like us."

"Smart. I agree Mange won't be one of the regular bowlers either unless he follows us and takes over one of their bodies." That thought caused her to shiver.

Thane slammed a palm on the wheel. "Jeez. All the more reason I need to kill him."

"We'll kill him together."

He looked over at her. "Yes, together."

When they arrived, Angelique was a bit put off to have to rent shoes others had worn. At least Thane had told her she'd need socks, so she came somewhat prepared.

"I suggest we grab a bite to eat at the bar and watch the pros before we try this game. We might be able to pick up a pointer or two."

Thane really seemed to want them to succeed. "I've not had the chance to play games before."

He ran a knuckle down her cheek. "We'll just have to change that, won't we? I have faith you'll do great. You picked up on the fighting techniques rather quickly."

She smiled. "I did at that. I also wasn't too bad on the obstacle course either."

He smiled. "You were amazing, though part of me believes you must have used a little magic. No one makes it over those five barrels on the first try."

Angelique opened her mouth in an exaggerated fashion. "I did not cheat." Two could play at this game. "I didn't realize you had such a fragile ego."

His eyes widened. "I most certainly do not."

"You do too. When I almost beat you the first time, you couldn't stand that I might be as coordinated as you."

Thane laughed. "We'll see about that shortly, won't we?"

Thane escorted her to the food counter. Together, they checked out the menu items that ranged from burgers to pizza—something Thane said came from Earth a long time ago."

"How about we share a pizza?" she suggested.

"Great idea. What kind do you want?"

After a back and forth discussion, they picked something with mostly vegetables. "Since I don't sense Mange here, how about a beer?" she asked.

Thane smiled. "A woman after my own heart."

After they enjoyed the simple meal and a cold drink, it was time to bowl—and time to prove to Thane she was his equal. She might not be able to fly, but she had her talents.

Picking the right ball was quite a challenge, but she swore having mated with Thane made her stronger than ever.

Once at their lane, she studied the other players. "Do you sense any shifters?" she asked, curious how good his shifter sensors were.

"A few. Those on lane 3 seem to be dragon shifters, but lane 4 is a combination of humans and what I am sensing are wolf shifters. When there are a lot of people around, the signals can become jumbled."

"Good to know." Learning about Thane was fun. "Did you play a lot of organized sports growing up?" She had no idea what most kids did.

"Remember, I've been around for over a hundred years. When I was a young pup, we kicked a ball around, but that's about all. Not many traveled to Earth in those days, so we didn't pick up on their games. I've been there recently, so I've watched basketball, baseball, and soccer, but it wasn't something we did."

She rubbed his arm. "Were you forced into protecting others from a young age?"

Thane faced her and cupped her shoulders. "There was no forcing. We are born with the need to care for others, a need to protect. It was almost like Fate gave us powers to sense when someone is in trouble, but we're all different. I, for one, have a talent for battle."

"I'm glad you can protect yourself and others. Since Declan and Greer are healers, I'm assuming that's their special talent?"

"Yes. They have other abilities too though. We're all multi-talented." Thane smiled.

"That makes sense. Since you seem to all fight a lot, Declan and Greer must be called into action frequently."

"Not really. Our dragons have healing powers above and beyond the average dragon." He tapped her nose. "But enough questions for now. Besides, this isn't the place for that kind of discussion."

Shit. She forgot that people didn't know who the Guardians were. "Sorry."

He stilled. "You have nothing to be sorry about. You wanted to learn about me, and I appreciate that. Now let's put on our shoes."

Angelique sat on the bench and slipped on her ugly bowling shoes. From the screen above them, the score was calculated automatically, for which she was glad. "Why don't you go first?" she said, not wanting to make a fool of herself.

"Okay, but I hope you won't feel bad when I knock down all the pins on my first try."

She'd never seen him joke like this before. "I'll be cheering for you."

Thane picked up the ball, and like the others nearby, took three steps and then rolled the ball down the alley with incredible power. The similarity between him and others stopped there. Halfway down the lane, the ball went into the gutter.

He spun around. "This lane must be crooked."

She cracked up. "I'm sure, but you're a Sinclair. You can adjust."

He seemed happy about her concession. "You're right."

Too bad on the next throw, the ball only nicked one pin, but to his credit, he didn't pout. Now she saw what Thane was really made of. He was a good sport.

Angelique jumped up. "My turn."

She didn't have as big of an ego, so there was no reason to throw the ball as hard as she could just to show off. With slow control, Angelique rolled the ball down the middle of the lane. She was so excited until only the pins in the middle fell down.

Thane clapped. "Nice job."

While she scored better than he did, she'd never be able to knock them all down. "I'll do better next time."

Her second throw unfortunately went right through the middle again.

Thane puffed out his chest. "I've figured this out now. Be prepared to be wowed."

She laughed, just as he probably intended. His next throw was actually good, knocking down eight pins. Excited for his success, she ran up the lane and threw her arms around his neck.

Thane smiled. "You're easy to please, I see."

"I think you should be rewarded for your prowess."

"Is that so? Just what are you willing to do now that half the bowling alley is watching?"

Heat raced up her face as she turned to look around. Sure enough, about eight people were staring at them—and thankfully smiling. She lightly kissed him and then stepped back, but that little bit excited her white light. When she glowed, Angelique rushed back to the seat. She didn't need all of Tarradon finding out what she was—a light entity from another realm. Glowing dragon scales were one thing, but a whole body glow was another.

Thane grinned. "Be good now!"

With a very hard toss, Thane clipped the side of the pin on the left that then slid across the lane and knocked over the other. She jumped up and cheered. While she was highly competitive, she decided that Thane might indeed be the better bowler.

It seemed as if once Thane understood the game, he was willing to forgo the competition and just have a good time. One time he actually faced backward and tossed the ball between his legs. She swore he used some magic to make the it hit to the right of the head pin and knock them all down.

For fun, she decided to use some of her hidden talents. Hell, if she could stop an elevator, she certainly could make a ball go in the right direction.

"Stand aside, big boy. Angelique is here."

Thane bowed. She laughed.

Holding the ball to her chest, she then threw it extra hard. As it headed for the gutter, she said a spell to make it curve to the left, directly toward the sweet spot. Boom! Every pin fell.

A second later, Thane had her in his arms spinning her around. "That was awesome. Bet you can't do it again."

She whispered in his ear. "I can do it every time if I want."

He set her down. "You cheated?"

"You said you wanted to learn about me. I'm showing you what

I can do."

He leaned in closer. "Have you ever used magic in bed?"

"No! I never put any spells on you if that's what you are asking."

He winked. "Maybe you should try."

"How about after this game, we see what else I can do?"

His lips hovered over hers. "I say we leave now."

His eyes went from whisky brown to bright teal in a flash. To say his body looked like a gold plated statue was an understatement. As fast as they could, they ditched their shoes, returned their balls to the rack, and raced out of there.

Angelique's imagination went wild. She waved a hand at the car to make windows tint black. "Now, we'll have privacy," she said.

Thane laughed. *"You read my mind,"* he telepathed.

"Not really, but then I've never tried."

"That's a scary thought."

Thane opened her door, and instead of getting in, she shoved him into the passenger side seat. Before he could question her, she straddled him and then closed the door. Because it was highly cramped inside, she closed her eyes and made the car expand in every direction.

"How did you do that?"

She enjoyed how he always seemed surprised at her talents. "When I want something, I just make it happen—within reason, of course."

"Do I have that power now that we've mated?"

"I don't know, but if you're good, I might teach you."

"I can't wait."

She loved his light side—and his dark side—and every side of this man. "Just shut up and kiss me."

Thane must have used some magic of his own, because he managed to kiss her and undo her shorts at the same time.

Not having the patience for him to wiggle out of his jeans, she levitated him, and dragged his pants down over his butt. Gotta love a man who goes commando.

"Whoa. That was impressive," Thane said, his tone laced with appreciation.

He reached around her and lowered his pants past his knees, while she managed to ditch her shorts and panties.

Unable to hold out any longer, she kissed him again. He opened up and welcomed her in. Their tongues darted in and out, mimicking what she really wanted to do with another body part. He dragged his fingers through her hair, tugging and pressing hard. The more they kissed, the more pressure he used, igniting her further.

Their breaths mingled, and their energy united. It was as if they were the only two people in the world.

With her free hand, she reached between them and grabbed his dick. Because she was already slick, Angelique slid his cock straight into her.

Thane stiffened. "Holy shit. You have no idea how good you feel."

"Not as good as you feel inside me."

As if their animal sides took over, Angelique rode him hard. This didn't seem to be as much about tender loving right now as pure unadulterated need. With each thrust, her desire built. For a moment, she swore her body's white glow had been tinted with pink, but that wasn't possible. She'd been told she could never shift, but maybe the deities had been wrong. Thane was so powerful she could almost feel his dragon building a life inside her.

He broke the kiss and leaned her back then slid his mouth to her throat. "Shirt has to go," he mumbled.

Together, they lifted it off her. With a quick pinch, her bra was history. A second later, his lips were on her breasts, and sparks of need consumed her. When Thane leaned forward, she dragged her hands down his back. While being in a bed would have been more comfortable, she couldn't have waited any longer. Every suck and touch sent her higher.

"Kiss me again," she demanded.

As if her wish was his command, Thane sat up taller and complied. He framed her face and kissed her with more hunger than she'd ever known before. Their tongues curled around each other, and she savored the slight tomato and beer taste from their dinner.

Using his right hand, Thane tilted the seat back to give them a little more room. He then grabbed her hips, held her still, and drove up into her. She dropped her head back and sucked in air. The magnitude of each violent thrust nearly toppled her. Angelique gripped his shoulders and screamed his name as her orgasm claimed her.

Seconds later, his cum filled her, but the pulsing and throbbing kept going. Exhausted, she collapsed her head onto his shoulder. With her last bit of effort, she managed to say a spell to return the car to its original small size.

What seemed like minutes later, someone pounded on their car roof. "Get a room."

It sounded like several boys who were laughing and whooping it up. Only slightly embarrassed, Angelique sat up as much as she could. "Maybe we should get dressed."

"Just maybe."

Chapter Fifteen

T HE NEXT WEEK was actually fairly calm. There had been no Mange sightings or deaths attributed to him. Angelique wasn't so naïve to believe that he'd left. No, he'd come here for a reason, and she doubted he'd just leave.

Once Josh Gerrard had declared her restaurant safe, she and the girls had been busy ordering new equipment and supervising the clean-up. As terrible as it had looked and smelled, the workers had performed a miracle. The new kitchen was a lot nicer than the original one, and the fresh paint job really perked up the coffee shop. If it hadn't been for Thane's insistence on helping to pay for some of the repairs, she didn't know when she could have opened. The insurance money didn't cover all of the repairs.

True to Thane's word, she'd had at least two, if not three, body-guards at her store the whole time, though she didn't believe they needed to be there. She let them stay because the girls seemed calmer with them there. To keep Mange from becoming suspicious why several burly men were at the coffee shop, she made them work by scraping wallpaper and washing countertops. Thankfully, none of them complained.

"When will you be opening again?" Griffin asked, his forehead beaded with sweat.

"In a couple of days."

He smiled. "You should have a grand re-opening party. In case he didn't mention it, Thane's birthday is coming up soon. We could celebrate both events at the same time."

"That's a great idea." Though she'd have a private birthday party first!

Considering what a bad cook she was, her greatest gift to him would be learning to make something he'd enjoy and appreciate.

"Angelique?" Shannon called.

"Coming." She turned back to Griffin. "More decisions to make."

Wanting her coffee shop to be nicer than before the fire, she, Melissa, and Shannon sat in the office to brainstorm ideas about which improvements would make the most impact. Besides the new paint job, they opted for bright gold curtains—a color she'd grown very fond of since arriving in Edendale.

Just as they finished with their list, Griffin poked his head in the office. "There's someone here to see you."

"Who is it?"

"Donald."

Joy raced through her. While her cook's injuries hadn't been life threatening, he wasn't a young man anymore. She rushed into the main room, thrilled he didn't possess Mange's evil signature.

"How are you?" she asked as she hugged him.

"Ready to get back to work. I'm not built to sit around and do nothing, you know."

The slice on his forehead had healed nicely, and the portion of his hair his doctors had shaved in order to stitch him up, had started to grow back. "If you're ready to work, I'm sure the kitchen can use your touch."

Donald grinned and then looked around. "I have to say, you wouldn't know there had been a fire here."

That was the best compliment he could have given her. "I had a lot of help."

"I can see."

With a glint in his eye, Donald headed back to the kitchen. Just maybe things would get back to normal soon.

"I'M SO HAPPY you called, Angelique," Thane's mother said.

They were in Moira's kitchen, and Angelique was really nervous, in part because she'd called Thane's mom to ask for her help. "Since it's Thane's birthday next week, I want to make him one of his favorite meals."

"That's sweet of you. I take it things are going well for you two?" Moira handed Angelique an apron to put on.

Weren't they supposed to go well? "Yes. Thane is wonderful."

His mom smiled. "Yes, he is, but he's often too serious. He feels responsible for all of us, and I keep telling him we don't need to train all the time."

That made Angelique laugh. "Thane is rather relentless. I'm still sore from our training sessions."

Moira stopped. "I thought he told me you couldn't shift."

"I don't think I can, but he wants to build up my endurance so I'll be ready for the likes of that horrible dark entity, Mange."

"I am so sorry about that. Has he struck again?"

Angelique wasn't sure if she'd heard about the elevator scare or not. "Not since the incident with Greer. Though I suspect this Mange was involved with the fire at my place."

"I am sorry what happened to you. That was terrible." His mom shook her head. "And Greer? Poor thing. She must have been petrified. I know I would have been if the elevator I was in fell."

Angelique remembered being impressed with how calm Thane's cousin had been. "If she was afraid, she didn't show it."

Moira smiled. "That's Greer for you. She looks fragile because of her delicate bone structure, but she is strong. And tough."

"I believe it."

"As to Thane's favorite meal, it's changed over the years." His mom inhaled. "The kids don't come over for dinner very often, but when Thane does, he loves his meat pie."

Angelique was a bit disappointed that he never talked about dinner with his parents or this meat pie. "What's in it?"

"Special stuff." His mom smiled. "I'll write down the recipe, but we'll make it now. Jamison loves it too, so we'll have a wonderful dinner tonight."

"I heard you all celebrate birthdays in this realm."

"We do for the special ones. Since we live so long, we get together every ten years. Between all of the Sinclairs and the Caspians, it seems as if we celebrate a birthday every six months."

Now she wished she'd had a family to share something like that with, though she had no idea when she started life as a ray of light.

Moira cupped her shoulder. "Jamison and Thane told me about your background. It must have been tough not having a family."

She smiled, though it took some effort. "I had a family of sorts. All light entities bond with each other. We might not have had a body, but we were born with a soul and a mind. We know what love is and learned the difference between good and evil."

Moira looked off to the side as if this was too much to understand. "Now that you're with us, the Sinclairs are your family."

Her kind words brought tears to her eyes. "Thank you."

Thane's mom dragged her hands down her apron. "Let's begin."

For the next half hour, his mom showed her how to blend spices into what looked like some kind of mixed chopped meat. After making it into a large patty, she topped the dish with tomatoes, mushrooms, and cheese. It seemed easy enough.

"While this bakes, we'll make some of his favorite side dishes."

One was a tomato and cheese hors d'oeuvre, and the other was a mix of chopped vegetables. If she knew cooking was this easy, Angelique would have tried it a while ago.

"I think I can do this," Angelique said.

"I'm sure you can. I'll write it down anyway, but call me if you are stuck."

"I will. My last attempt at cooking was a disaster. I burnt the toast, and the bacon came out tough."

Moira smiled. "You must have used the toaster in the safe house. That lever always sticks."

Thane was so lucky to have such a wonderful and understanding mom. Just as his mother was finishing writing down the recipe, Angelique's heart fluttered, and she pressed a palm to her chest.

Moira was by her side in a flash. "Is something wrong?" Thane's mom asked.

"My blood feels like it's racing through my veins, making my heart beat way too fast," Angelique said as she tried to slow her breathing.

"Is it coming from you or Thane?"

"I can't tell." She inhaled. *"Thane, are you hurt?"* she telepathed.

"Not me, but I just found out something has happened to Greer."

"What happened?" The pain radiating from Thane's voice actually hurt her.

"She's gone."

When Angelique's knees almost gave way, Moira clasped her shoulder to steady her. "What is it?"

"Thane told me Greer is gone."

"Gone, how? Is she dead?"

"Is Greer dead?" Angelique almost didn't want to ask.

"I hope not, but she's missing."

She'd never heard Thane sound this desperate before. *"Where are you?"*

"At the jewelry store. There's been a break-in."

Despite that bad news, it gave her hope that the thief had merely kidnapped Greer, though she had no idea why she thought that. *"I'll be right there."*

"Good."

Angelique faced Moira and told her what she knew, wanting to comfort her. "I'm sure Greer will be okay."

"You make sure my son lets me know if they find out anything. Poor Iona. If anything happens to Greer, it will kill my sister."

"I'm sure Greer will be fine. She can handle herself." Given Angelique's background, she had never been the demonstrative type, but more and more she craved the contact. She hugged Thane's mom goodbye. "Thank you for helping me."

Moira swiped her eyes and stepped over the counter. "Here's the recipe. Good luck."

The act of talking about food made the horror of what happened seem less real. "Thank you for everything."

Angelique rushed out of the house. What she wouldn't give to be able to fly, but her car would have to do.

The traffic seemed extra heavy today, or else it was that Angelique needed a lot more practice at driving. When she neared the SinCas building, Avonbelle police cars were everywhere with colorful flashing lights lighting up nearby windows. Two blocks later, she found a spot, parked, and ran back to the building.

"Ma'am," one of the policemen said. "This is a crime scene. You can't go in there."

She could argue with him, but that would take time. Just as she was about to mentally contact Thane, his cousin Anderson Caspian rushed down the street.

"Anderson?" she called.

He tossed her a weak smile. "Angelique. You shouldn't be here."

"Thane called and asked me to come. I might be able to sense if Mange was here." That was a stretch, but she'd say anything to be with Thane in his moment of need.

He nodded. "Of course. I have no idea if this is his doing or not. Can you tell me if he leaves any kind of residual aura, so to speak?"

"I'm not sure. I don't have all that much experience with him."

"Let's give it a try anyway."

The front window of the jewelry store was intact. If a theft occurred, and if Mange had been involved, he would have had to invade someone else's body. Damn.

As soon as Anderson led her inside, the angry and worried vibes from Thane still vibrated inside her. He spun around and rushed over to her. The hug that followed was warm and comforting, but it also held desperation.

"You came. Thank you," he said.

"Of course I did. What happened?" All of the damage seemed to be contained to one glass counter that had been smashed. The contents of the case were in disarray, making it hard to tell what might have been taken.

"I'm not sure, but they found one of Greer's red shoes on the floor."

Just one? The image of the same red shoe in the back of the elevator appeared in her mind's eye. "She needs to buy a different size. They seem to fly off her feet too often." While the situation was highly serious, something about that thought lightened her heart.

"That's the truth. At least we know she is alive."

He couldn't know that for sure. However, if they'd killed her during the robbery, they wouldn't have taken the body. Something didn't add up though. "If she was alive, why not shift into her dragon form and fight them off. I thought you told me you've trained every one of your relatives."

"I have, and Greer is formidable."

"If she's that good, how hard could it have been to take down the thief, even if he was a dragon shifter?"

Thane dragged a hand down his jaw. "There are several possibilities. One is that there were a number of thieves. Besides, she couldn't shift inside the building. The most likely scenario is that he, or rather they, drugged her."

Angelique's shoulders sagged. She looked between Thane and Anderson. "Do you think Mange could have done this?"

"I don't know. Is that his modus operandi?" Anderson asked.

"I wish I knew." She clearly didn't know enough about this dark entity.

Thane's cell rang. "Just a sec. Yes?" He turned his back and paced. Ever since they'd mated, her hearing had improved dramatically, but she honestly didn't want to listen to any more bad news.

Thane disconnected. "What is it?" Angelique asked, sensing some relief.

"That was one of my security team members. He has a clear picture of the man's face on video."

"We need to check it out," Anderson said.

"I'd like to see the video too. Not that I can tell if Mange has taken over the man's body, but I want to memorize his face—assuming he doesn't take another man's body soon."

"Sure." Thane stabbed a hand over his head. "Come on. The video room is down in the basement. We'll use the stairs instead of the elevator. I don't trust this ass."

"I don't either," Angelique said.

Anderson turned to Thane. "I don't remember a break-in before, unless you never reported it."

Thane bristled. "There has never been a robbery at SinCas until now. We have excellent security—security I oversee."

"Have you figured out yet what was taken?" Anderson asked.

Thane shook his head. "I called Tory to come down and take inventory."

During the rest of the trip to the basement, Thane kept quiet, but Angelique had a hard time breathing with all of his pain radiating inside her. After striding down the long hallway, Thane burst into the last room on the right. Inside sat a bank of monitors.

"Chris, can you show us what you found?" Thane asked.

"Sure." He pressed some buttons.

The video showed Greer buzzing in some nice looking guy wearing a navy blue suit. His dark hair was cut short, and he carried himself with confidence. He said something to Greer and then stuck his hand in his pocket. His eyes widened. A second later, he withdrew what looked like a syringe and stabbed Greer in the neck.

"What the hell?" Anderson said. "There was no provocation. Nothing."

Angelique's heart was beating so fast from the horror that Thane stepped back a bit and wrapped an arm around her waist. "Is there any sound?" she managed to ask.

"No. Strictly video," Thane told her. He turned to his cousin. "Do you know who the guy is?"

"Yes, but I can't believe it. His name is Blake Masters."

The next video showed Greer collapsing onto the floor. What happened after that was the oddest thing Angelique had ever seen. The man smashed the glass counter—a counter that would take extraordinary strength to break—with his fist, shattering it.

He then grabbed only a couple of items before dashing around the counter and picking up Greer. With her cradled in his arms, he ran out of the camera's view.

"That doesn't make any sense. Blake is an upstanding banker. In fact, the guy comes from a wealthy family. There is no reason for him to steal," Anderson said.

"And yet he did," Thane said.

"I don't understand why he took Greer with him." If this was Mange, he was acting very strangely.

"Can you pick them up from the hallway cameras?" Anderson asked.

"I'll try."

After a little searching, Chris found the hallway feed where Blake had Greer. Two seconds into the video, the screen filled with static. "Shit," Chris said.

"What happened?" Thane asked.

"I can't be sure, but it looks as if some electrical interference cut out the feed."

She grabbed Thane's arm. "If Mange shoots his dark light into something electrical, it can do some damage. That gives some credence to Mange having taken over Blake's body."

"Dear goddess in heaven. The poor man is going to die." Thane faced her. "Is there any way Mange can leave a body without killing his host?"

"I was able to enter and exit Declan when we fought Sanditra, so I see no reason why Mange can't do the same. The problem is, he'll have no reason to do so."

Chapter Sixteen

THANE WAS FURIOUS and scared. If Mange had been the one who'd taken Greer, what did he want with her? Was this his sick way of luring Angelique somewhere and then trying to harm her?

She rubbed his shoulder. "It is possible Mange wasn't responsible, though the chance of that is slim."

They were now upstairs in one of the offices because Thane needed a computer to search the Internet. Anderson had headed back to the station.

"Maybe." Though he wasn't inclined to believe it. "Do you think this upstanding banker—what was his name?"

"Blake Masters."

Clearly, he was losing it. "Yes, Blake Masters. If Mange isn't involved, are you thinking he acted on his own?" She must know something about Mange that she wasn't telling him.

Angelique shrugged. "I know nothing about the man, but I think we should keep our options open. Is there a surveillance video of Masters on the way to the store? I'm not sure if I can tell when Mange enters a body, but perhaps there is some physical manifestation we missed."

Ah, so that was her concern. "Smart thinking. I should have thought of that. We pay the shop across the street to allow us to keep our cameras on their building. They face the jewelry store. Let's go downstairs and ask Chris to pull up the feed."

Once there, Chris located the spot on the video, but all it showed was Blake heading toward SinCas. He stopped in front of the door and rang the bell. "Everything looks ordinary," Thane said.

"Can you play it again, Chris?" Angelique asked.

"Sure." He queued it up again.

"What caught your attention?" Thane asked.

"I'm not sure." She leaned closer toward the screen. "There. Stop it."

"What is it?"

"I can't be sure, but see the man with the red curly hair wearing a brown suit?"

"Yes. What about him?

"It's hard to tell, but it appears as if he just placed something in Blake's pocket."

"Like a reverse pick pocket?" Thane asked.

"Exactly."

"Why would someone do that?" he asked.

"Greer was stabbed with a syringe. Maybe this guy dropped it into Masters' pocket," Angelique said.

Thane asked Chris to slow down the feed. The problem was that the man's back was to the camera, preventing them from identifying him, but it was clear that his arm moved forward. "Chris, can we find a better picture that shows the man's face?"

"I'll try."

Just as the image of the man with red hair and a beard appeared, Thane's cell rang. It was Anderson. Shit. "What did you find out?"

"I think Mange is the thief and kidnapper."

"What proof do you have?"

"We just found a dead man in the alley behind the bank with a burn mark in his body where his hip used to be."

His mind spun. "Don't tell me this corpse has red hair and a beard."

"Holy fuck. He does. How do you know that?"

He told Anderson about the video. "I can't be certain, but it appears as if this red-headed man who was apparently possessed by Mange, put something—probably a syringe—into Blake Masters' pocket right before he entered the store."

"Why would he do that?" Anderson asked. "He couldn't be certain that Blake would look in his pocket or know what to do with it unless the two were in cahoots."

Angelique grabbed Thane's arm. "Put him on speaker."

"Anderson, it's Angelique."

"What is it?" Anderson asked.

"Do you remember when Blake stuck his hand in his pocket when he was standing in front of the counter?"

"Yes. He pulled out a syringe—possibly the one this bearded man gave him."

She inhaled. "Yes, but I just remembered how his eyes went wide—almost as if he had no idea the syringe was in there. Then his body stiffened slightly."

"What are you thinking?" Thane asked.

"That might have been when Mange entered Blake's body. He was in the body of the red headed man, and then he went into Blake's. To be sure, I'd like to see the footage again."

Thane wasn't buying it. "If Mange was in the bearded man's body, would he have had time to go behind the bank, exit his body, and then rush back to SinCas? All in about thirty seconds?"

"He is dark light, which travels quite fast, but it's possible he stopped time."

Thane's muscles bunched. This was too much to comprehend. "Stopped time? How is that possible?"

She held up her hands. "I can't do it, but I've seen some dark lighters with that ability. I'm not sure if Mange has the capability but it would explain how he could almost be in two places at once."

"Jeez," Anderson said. "We'll never get this guy."

"You can't think like that," Angelique said. "We will stop him. We just need to be smart"

"I thought we had been," Anderson said. "What's your theory on why Mange would need two bodies? Why not enter the store as this bearded man?"

"When I find Mange, I'll ask him," she said.

Anderson huffed out an exasperated sigh. "Good luck with that. By the way, I stopped by the bank where Blake Masters works. As expected, he didn't show up today. One of his coworkers said that he was planning on asking his girlfriend to marry him this weekend, which was why he was at the jewelry store—to buy an engagement ring."

"Have you spoken with his girlfriend?"

"Yes. She is devastated, of course. I asked if Blake had been acting strange, and she said no, nor had he ever been aggressive toward her. She swears he doesn't do drugs either."

"Were they having money problems?"

"Not at all. The girlfriend works at the hospital as an administrator. Together, they do well financially, and that's not even considering the family money he stands to inherit."

"It does seem as if Blake is a victim. I feel sorry for both of them," Thane said. "I still find it hard for Mange to be in both bodies at relatively the same time, unless he can stop time."

"I agree."

"If you learn anything new, keep us in the loop," Thane said.

"Will do."

Thane disconnected and faced Angelique. "Do you have any idea why he'd take Greer? Or where he might take her?"

"No. My guess is that he wants us to look for her. When we do, he'll try to take me down."

Thane stroked her cheek. "That's not going to happen. Good thing he has no way of knowing that we've mated."

"Unless he thinks he can get Greer to tell him."

Thane shook his head. "No. Greer will figure out who this person is. She won't tell him anything."

"I hope so." Angelique's eyes softened. "There is one silver lining to all of this."

"Which is?" Thane asked.

"I'm not sure we would have mated this soon if this mess hadn't happened."

Thane ran a knuckle down her cheek. "I wouldn't be so sure about that. I can be very persuasive when I want something."

He finally got the smile he wanted to see. "You got that right."

They headed back upstairs to the main level where they found Tori sifting through the contents of the case. She rushed over and hugged Thane. "This is so terrible. Who would do this to Greer?"

Thane filled her in on what they knew so far.

"How can we find this guy if he changes bodies all the time?" Tory asked.

"That is the big question."

Angelique pumped her fist twice. "I wish I knew how far away from Mange I need to be in order to sense him. If it's a couple hundred feet, we could fly over the city in the hopes I could tell where he is."

Thane placed a hand on her shoulder and squeezed. "When he attacked you at your house, you didn't sense him until he shot his darkness into you."

"Damn. You're right. Maybe I should broadcast to all of Avonbelle where I'll be and at what time in order for Mange to seek me out."

"No!" Thane shouted. "I bet that's what he wants."

"If you want to get your cousin back, we might have to lure him out."

"Over my dead body."

GREER WAS CERTAIN she had a thousand pound weight sitting on her chest. Not only was she having difficultly breathing, her eyelids refused to work. She thought she was able to wiggle her toes and fingers, but maybe it was only her imagination, especially when she tried to speak, and her mouth wouldn't move.

Think!

One minute she was about to show this hot man some rings, and the next she seemed to be encased in cement. She remembered him reaching out to her, and then something pierced her neck, sending heat through her veins. Had he drugged her or had there been a blast of some sorts, and she was actually trapped underground? Bits and pieces of her sister's exploits about when Nessa had been trapped hundreds of feet underground surfaced. If she could dig her way out, so could Greer.

Someone grunted—or at least she thought that was what it was—but when she held her breath to heighten her hearing, there was nothing but silence once more. Greer exhaled and then coughed, implying she really was alive. Slowly, her breaths came more easily. It was almost as if the weight was lifting.

Greer needed to wake up, but it was as if she'd been paralyzed. If she could have shivered from that horrific thought, she would have. Hopefully, she'd only been drugged and wasn't pinned under the rubble of a collapsed building. Drugs wore off, but buildings didn't levitate on their own.

Her senses were always her best attribute. She needed to use them now. Greer tried to catalog the odors to understand her surroundings better. It was a mixture of dampness and mold with something else—something that was kind of sweet and musky. Her first thought was that it was a man's cologne, but then she dismissed it. Unless…the man at the counter was here too, the man who she believed had done something to her.

She really needed to shift in order to fully heal. The problem was if she couldn't move, she couldn't shift. At least her brain seemed to be logically working. With a gargantuan effort, she finally opened her eyes. Now she wished she hadn't. Above her were bars. Around her were bars. Holy crap, she was in a cage maybe four feet long, three feet wide, and not more than three feet high. While terrified of her new situation, at least the presence of the man curled up outside her cage meant she wasn't alone.

Greer blinked to clear her vision. Wait a minute. He was the man from the store—the one who probably stabbed her in the neck.

He looked dead. Shit.

"Hello?" she called, hoping he was merely unconscious. Thankfully, her mouth moved and sound came out—kind of.

No answer. That wasn't good.

With a great deal of effort, she rolled onto one side. Her muscles were stiff but nothing seemed to be broken. Her dragon must have been working all along. "Are you alive?" she asked.

Greer felt a little crazy talking to what looked like a dead man, but she needed to know whether he was a threat. Guardians were trained to assess the situation. After scooting closer to the edge of the cage, she reached her hand through the bars and nudged him. A spark seemed to jump from him to her that was actually pleasurable. Okay, that was odd, but she didn't have the luxury of figuring it out. She had to get out of there.

When he grunted, Greer froze, not knowing if she should be happy he was alive or scared he'd do more damage to her. After all, someone had put her in a cage. Whatever he had or hadn't done, she doubted this man meant to end up like this. It was possible he was a pawn too.

Or was he? The more she replayed what happened, the more certain she was that this man had stabbed her in the neck. Considering what little she did remember, it had to have been a sedative—a very strong one.

Before she spent more time figuring out who was behind this mess, she studied her environment. The cage and this man were in a fairly large empty building the size of a warehouse. The only windows were about twenty feet above the floor, perfect for a dragon shifter to look out of. The problem was that Greer couldn't shift until she escaped from the cage, and shifting while confined would cause her some damage. If this man awoke though, he might be able to call for help—or else he'd find a way to keep her caged forever.

Chapter Seventeen

ANGELIQUE HAD NEVER seen Thane so upset before, but she totally understood why he was troubled. His cousin was missing.

Angelique rubbed his shoulder. "Greer is a Guardian. She is also aware of who, or rather what, Mange is. She'll figure something out."

"That's all well and good, but all Mange has to do is enter her body, use her for whatever terrible deed he wants, and then kill her, like he has with all of his other victims."

Her heart sank. "There has to be something we can do."

"Anderson, half the police force, and many of the Guardians, are out looking for her."

Angelique paced in front of him. "We don't know if Mange is still in Masters' body or if he's taken another victim."

"Let's hope he has left Blake—leaving Greer to escape—but I don't know why he would."

"He has to know we'll have him on surveillance," Angelique said.

"Which is all the more reason he needs to find another person to take over."

"What are Griffin, Logan, Birk, and Camden doing right now? And Nessa. She has to be beside herself too."

Thane glared out the window as if he hoped to spot Mange or his cousin. "They're combing the area. The police are doing the same. If anyone senses or sees anything, they will contact us. Everyone knows not to try to take Mange down."

"Good. We don't need more deaths."

Tory came over to Thane with a list. "This is what was taken. It isn't much."

Thane scanned the missing jewelry items. "I think he wanted it to look like a heist, but I don't think the theft was his main target."

Angelique nodded. "I agree, which points to Mange more than anyone."

"Because?" Thane asked.

"You don't rob a jewelry store unless you know how to unload the pieces. Mange won't have any idea how to sell them. Like myself, there are things we are rather naïve about—like fencing stolen goods. Also, if it were just a robbery, why would he drug and take Greer with him?"

"You're right." Thane snapped his fingers. "His next target could be another jewel thief or a fence to help him get rid of the items."

She liked his thinking, but it didn't help them much. "Are you planning to warn every fence in Edendale? What would you tell them?"

"Assuming a fence was willing to talk with us, we'll show them photos of the stolen items and just say the man selling them is very dangerous."

"I doubt the fence would live long enough to contact you once Mange finds him," she said. "My guess is that he'll just toss the jewels."

"You might be right." Thane escorted her over to one of the sofas near the front of the store and motioned she sit down. "As much as I want to look for Greer, a good portion of the town is out there doing just that. Mange might be waiting for us to get close before he pounces."

"And we'll be ready."

Thane leaned back and sighed. "I want to catch him on our own terms."

Thane was sweet but a little naïve. "How do you propose to do that?"

"Do what you suggested. Draw him out."

She hadn't seen that coming. "I thought you said that was a bad idea."

"I know, but I've changed my mind."

"What are you planning?" she asked.

"What if you and I take a little vacation? If Mange learns of our departure, he might leave Greer alone and come look for us."

Angelique blew out a breath, trying to remember what a dark entity might do in this situation. From what she'd learned in her time in the realm, dark entities like Mange were what humans called sociopaths. If she could, she'd return to her realm and ask those in the know that exact question. The problem was she wasn't sure she could come back. "I wish Fay Forrester understood dark entities."

"She might."

"It's doubtful. It sounds like she is a different kind of light being."

Thane placed her hand in his. "Even if we don't draw out Mange, it might do us some good to get away. One night alone would do wonders."

Images of wild lovemaking filled her head. "Do you have a place in mind?"

"I do, but I need to set it up."

"If you want Mange to find us, you'll have to have someone leak the information. Who will you tell?"

He tapped his foot. "I'll suggest Anderson let his men know and then ask Griffin to tell all of the Guardians. I'm sure the word will spread fast."

She inhaled. "Let's do this."

"IF THE REASON we are here weren't so serious, I'd have to thank Mange," Angelique said, looking around. "I've never seen a house in a tree before. Is it safe?"

Thane chuckled. "Very. Let's drop off our backpacks, and then I'll show you the best part."

She thought this was the best part. "Do you own this?"

"No. Anderson's parents own it."

"How is he related to you, exactly?"

Thane pointed to the ladder. "Climb up, and I'll tell you once we are inside."

The house was about twenty feet above the ground. As soon as she stepped onto the wooden deck, her heart fluttered. Completely surrounded by trees, there were two rocking chairs on the porch. She stepped inside the tree house and was amazed by how much it looked like a real home. Along the far wall was a kitchen, complete with sink, a burner stove, and a small refrigerator. In the middle of the room was a gloriously big four-poster bed with mosquito netting all around it. The windows were made of glass, but they opened up to fully embrace the out of doors.

"How do you like it?" Thane asked.

"I can't imagine Mange ever finding us. He'd have to inhabit a dragon shifter's body just to fly here."

He pulled her close. "That's okay by me if he doesn't locate us. That way I can have you all to myself."

"Don't you feel guilty not searching for Greer?"

"Hell, yes I do, but I think she'll be better off if we aren't around. It's the best way to force Mange to leave her. I know Greer. She'll figure something out."

Angelique actually understood his logic. When Chelsea had been captured, Thane had been by Declan's side, searching for her for hours. A wolf shifter was no match to a dark lighter. Greer however was a dragon shifter with other talents.

Angelique slipped off her backpack that contained her clothes, toiletries, and some food, in awe they were in such a quiet, peaceful place. She spun toward him. "Thank you for suggesting this."

Thane moved closer. "It's my pleasure." He swatted her butt. "Come on, I want to show you something."

"What is it?"

"You'll see." Back down the ladder they went. "I hope you're up for a little hike."

"Always. Plus, it will build my endurance."

"That's my girl."

"You said you'd tell me how Anderson and you are related."

"My mom and Griffin's mom are sisters, which makes all of the Sinclairs and Caspians first cousins. Griffin's dad's brother is Anderson's father. While my family isn't related to Anderson in the sense of being connected by blood, our magic unites us. We treat each other like cousins."

"I think I understand, but it's complicated." Figuring out where everyone fit in the family tree was hard.

"It is a little. Just so you know, we'll be heading east for a bit," he said.

To be honest, she thought *for a bit* meant they'd walk a mile or two on a relatively flat surface—not climb a freaking mountain. Thane seemed to be some mountain man who could defy gravity. While Angelique huffed and puffed—and slipped more than once—they finally reached the pinnacle almost two hours later. She had never been more proud of an accomplishment.

"Turn around," Thane said.

When Angelique looked back where they'd climbed, her heart nearly stopped. "This is incredible. I can see for miles."

"It is beautiful. I haven't been up here in years, but this area of Avonbelle has always been special to me. But there's more."

"More?"

Thane smiled. "I'll show you."

"Is it far?"

He laughed. "No. Now that we're mated, you're not going to turn into a wimp on me, are you? Because if you do, I'll have to kick your ass until you shape up."

Before she could defend herself, he kissed her and all thoughts of what he'd just said flew out of her head. Only because she was a bit sweaty did she pull back. "Maybe we should wait until we return to the tree house to indulge in any kind of carnal pleasure."

"You won't have to wait that long." Thane winked.

What did that mean? If she'd learned one thing about Thane, he loved to challenge and then surprise her. "Lead on, my macho man."

Thane puffed out his chest. "It's really not far."

Twenty not-so-short minutes later, they came to a cluster of trees. "What is this place? I hear water."

"Push aside the tree limbs and step inside the small copse."

When she moved aside the branches, she entered a magical land. It wasn't like her light realm, but it seemed just as unreal. To the left stood a ten-foot tall waterfall that spilled into a small pond with steam rolling off the surface. "What is this place?"

"It's a hot spring that I bet very few people know about. The best part is that while the water is quite warm, if you need to cool off, you have the waterfall to stand under."

"It's kind of like the grotto, except I can't see the bottom."

"It is like that."

Angelique remained still, enjoying the richly aromatic frenlen trees, the slight sulfur smell of the heated water, and the musky loam of the ground. "We don't have anything like this in our realm." She opened her eyes. "Actually, our realm is nothing other than light. Thank you for bringing me here."

Thane dragged a knuckle down her cheek and smiled. "I have to admit I had an ulterior motive."

From the way his teeth had sharpened and his whisky colored eyes had morphed into the color of the pool water, she could guess what was on his mind—the same thing that was on hers.

Considering all that had happened, she hadn't expected Thane to want to have sex with her because his dragon would be too overwrought to consider pleasure. Clearly, Angelique had been wrong.

"What is your motive?" Angelique stepped closer, cupped the back of his head, and dragged his lips to hers.

His answer came in the form of action. Their tongues became one as they explored each other. Sometime during the kiss, his hands found the button on her waistband. Once he unhooked it, he slipped down her pants.

For many reasons, she wanted to take a dip in the pool first before having wild, uninhibited sex. "Let me help."

Angelique took off her shoes and socks and then ditched her shorts, shirt, and bra. She'd let Thane deal with her panties.

Dropping to his knees, he slowly eased them down to her ankles. Thane pressed his face to her pussy as he grabbed her ass and squeezed. "I could stay here all day."

"I might not be a shifter, but I swear there is a dragon inside of me roaring for you to take me."

He leaned back. "It can't be anything like what my dragon is doing to me. He's more demanding than ever before."

She grinned. "It must be all of my sexy white light that is urging him on."

Thane rose to his feet. "I guess I better do what he's begging me to do."

It took him only seconds to ditch his clothes. Angelique admired his big cock, which was standing at attention.

"I hope the hot water doesn't bother him. I have a very good use for him."

"Trust me, he'll always be standing for your attention."

She loved the way Thane could always put a positive spin on everything. "Let's give it a try."

Not knowing how deep the pool was, she sat on the edge and eased in. While it wasn't cold out, the hot water was actually refreshing. To her delight, her feet touched the sandy bottom just as the water covered her breasts.

Thane slid in next to her. "I've dreamed of doing this from the first moment I met you."

"I'm glad you insisted we come here."

"Me too."

She smiled as she grabbed his cock. "Try not to distract me too much. I have to be on alert for you know who."

He pulled her closer. "You seem to forget that I too am full of white light. I bet I can sense his darkness now also."

She almost sagged with relief knowing she'd have help. "You should be able to, for which I am grateful." Squeezing his hard shaft, she pumped her fist. "Because we can sense if Mange is nearby—which he isn't at the moment—how about we forget our troubles for a little bit and grab some enjoyment while we can?"

"Seems to me you're holding a fistful of joy already."

Angelique cracked up and let go of his dick. "You are a funny man, Thane Sinclair."

He gave her a rather fake pout. "Don't let anyone hear you say that."

"Are you worried it will sully your tough guy reputation?"

"Damn right, woman."

Before she could comment, Thane lifted her up by her butt, dipped his head, and sucked on a very wet tit.

"You are so going down, Sinclair," she said.

He lifted his head. "I'm counting on it."

Chapter Eighteen

SOMEHOW THANE LANDED on his back on the needle-covered ground with leaves in his hair and the woman of his dreams straddling him. Had she tossed him up there, or had he crawled out of the hot spring? Not that it mattered, but it seemed as if her touches and kisses made him forget everything.

"This is much better," Angelique said as she sat on him. "I needed more traction."

Thane reached out an arm and dragged his discarded shirt closer. In one quick move, he'd flipped them over with him on top of her. "I get a say so in this, you know."

She laughed. "And why is that?"

"Because you love it when I dominate you."

Angelique glowed from within. "What are you waiting for then?"

Thane pounced, sucking on her tits once more as he slid two fingers into her heated opening. Angelique gasped and grabbed his shoulders. Whoa. He slightly winced at the sharpness of her nails. Checking them out, he was stunned to find sharp talons had poked through her skin. What the hell? The ramification stunned him. Now wasn't the time to see if she'd inherited any other talents from him though. She must not have noticed, or Angelique certainly would have said something.

She dragged her palms up his neck and then scraped her nails over his head. Thankfully, their sharpness seemed to have dulled or else his thick scalp was a lot tougher than his shoulders.

"Angelique, everything about you is so incredible."

Her smile faltered as she wiggled her butt. "Your two fingers are pretty incredible too."

Keeping his fingers inside her, Thane slid up and kissed her. Instead of devouring each other, he swept his tongue inside her mouth until she met his with cautious teasing. As if they had a hundred years to explore each other, he caressed her mouth with slow languorous strokes. With each twist and thrust, his heat grew, making Thane fear his dragon might not behave himself.

I will be good if you finish the job, his sassy dragon said.

Keep quiet, and let me enjoy her.

Angelique rubbed his back and then lifted her hips. More often than he'd like, they gave into their urges too quickly. This time he wanted to spend time enjoying every inch of the woman he loved. He slipped his fingers out of her, and she moaned.

Not wanting to lose contact, he dropped down between her legs, spread her feet wide, and settled in for his feast.

"I love your scent. It stirs my blood." To prove how much he wanted her, he dipped his head and swiped his tongue across her pussy.

"I feel heat," Angelique panted.

He hoped that didn't mean she planned to shift on him. Wouldn't that startle her? Thane placed his palm on her stomach and zeroed in on her slightly swollen clit. The rush of the waterfall, together with the steam rising off the hot spring, made their cocoon all the more perfect for loving his woman completely.

Angelique's moans grew louder and louder with every lick. His dick throbbed and pulsed, yearning to delve into her sweetness, but Thane was determined to hold out for as long as he could.

Take her now, his dragon urged.

I'll do this my way. Now shut up and let me enjoy her.

She lowered her hands to the ground and dug into the leaves and dirt. "Take me, please!"

Thane grunted his response as he reached up and plucked one nipple and then the other. "I can't get enough of you."

She grabbed a hunk of his hair. "Now!"

Thane loved a desperate, aggressive woman. Considering all she'd been through, he should give in to her demand. And it might shut up his dragon.

He rose to his knees, flipped her over, and lifted her to her knees. "Hold on for the ride of your life."

"I'm so ready."

While Thane's scales were flashing gold, patches of white light were shining through—a true sign that the two were united as one. As he leaned forward to guide his cock into her, a sprinkling of pink lit up her back—like dragon scales trying to form. Had he not been about to dive into her, Thane would have shouted for joy and demand they test out her potential skill.

He slid his hands up to her waist and plunged into her slickness. Angelique lowered her head and clawed the earth. She must be hanging on by a thread, because just as he was about to withdraw, Angelique leaned forward and then drove her hips back, encasing his dick. Sparks shimmied up his spine, as the scales on his back thickened.

Don't you dare shift, you horny bastard!

Then hurry, his dragon answered back.

Thane had prided himself on his control, but this wisp of a woman had completely undone him. Her white light blended with his dragon, making him whole and happy.

Reaching around her, Thane palmed her tits, pressing them together as he hammered into her again and again. With each stroke, his climax brimmed.

"Yes, Thane! Just like that."

Angelique's plea of greedy satisfaction shattered his control. He lowered his face to her neck and pressed his sharpened teeth against her skin. On the next thrust, he dug his teeth into her. Her scream, coupled with her inner walls grabbing his cock, made him come hard, fast, and powerful.

Angelique dropped to her elbows and pressed her forehead against his crumpled shirt. Their breaths came out labored, and

Thane never wanted to let her go.

He must not have been paying attention because one minute she was on her knees and the next on her stomach.

Thane rolled off her. "Did I squish you?"

With effort, she rolled over and smiled. "I don't think so."

She looked so cute with leaves in her hair and dirt on her elbows. "Anyone up for a nice warm dip?" he asked.

"If you lift me up."

In a flash, he had her in the water and cradled in his arms. "We need to come here more often."

She pushed her feet against the side and floated in the pool. "I guess there is no way to just fly here."

"Too many trees for that."

She stretched out her arms and patted the water. From the way her eyes fluttered, he feared she might fall asleep.

Thane slipped his hands under her body to keep her afloat.

"This is nice," she said, her voice trailing off.

Only when she started to prune did he decide it was time to return. "Come on water lady, we need to head on down."

She groaned. "It's a paradise here."

"I agree, but I need time to lightproof our tree house."

She dropped her feet to the bottom. "I never thought of that. If we lock the doors, a man wouldn't be able to get in, but light could. I like the way you think."

"I'm not a Guardian for nothing."

Thane levered himself out and then helped her. "Let's do this."

When the timing was right, he'd see if Angelique wanted to try to shift. Having her attempt it and fail might be too daunting right now. Once Mange was dead would be soon enough.

GREER WAS PISSED—MOSTLY at herself for not having faster reflexes to stop this guy from attacking her. She wracked her brain to remember if she'd seen him before today. He was a dragon shifter so she might have, but the question was where?

All she could recall about those few seconds from the moment she buzzed him in to the time he leaned over the counter was that her body had reacted quite favorably toward him—or rather lustfully—until he'd jammed that needle into her. Her heart had been beating really fast and there had been slight pressure from her talons, almost as if her animal wanted to escape. Once the drug reached her system, she blacked out.

Most likely she'd been confused about what her body was telling her. Her dragon must have recognized him as a threat and not as a possible lover.

Oh, shit. Was this man really Mange? It would make sense since the dark entity was evil. Hell, he'd already tried to harm her by messing with the elevator.

Something about all of this didn't seem right though. Thane said he never sensed that his friend Denalt was evil, but being a healer, she believed she'd be able to. After focusing on this person's aura for a solid minute, she sagged. She'd sensed nothing. Maybe the man outside her cage wasn't a dark lighter, but that didn't necessarily mean he was a victim either.

He was on his side with his back to her. His lack of movement implied he was still out cold. Carefully, she reached her hand between the bars and placed it on the man's shoulder, hoping to sense something from the contact. When a rash of tingles chased up her spine, she withdrew her hand fast. Something was happening, and she didn't like it one bit.

Greer's mind raced. Needing to push aside this man's guilt or innocence for the moment, she had to figure out a way to escape. One option was to extend her claws and shoot fire out the ends in an attempt to cut through the metal, but that would take a lot of time. Nessa would have had her out of there in a heartbeat since her sister's fire was extremely hot and had pinpoint accuracy. Greer didn't possess that level of talent.

She ran her hand on the outside of the cage until she found the lock. That would be the weakest point. Her second option was to send some of her healing power through this man in the hopes he'd help her, though why would he if he put her in the cage in the first place? Or had he?

What didn't fit was why he was unconscious. He might have been paid to harm her. It was possible that those in charge didn't want to leave any evidence behind and knocked him out too. The facts were clear. This man had come to a jewelry store to buy something, and ended up drugging her.

Once more, she reached through the bars and dug her hands into his jacket pocket looking for the key to the lock. Empty. Because he didn't seem aware she was frisking him, she rolled him onto his back in order to reach the other side. Only then did she see what looked like a brown stain around his midsection. Most likely it was dirt. This warehouse was anything but clean.

Greer grabbed his jacket and searched the other pocket as well as the inside one. All of them were empty. His pants pockets had nothing in them either. Given her incarceration, she thought he might have come in to rob the store, but he didn't have any jewels on him. Or had he taken them, and someone else had stolen them from him?

If he didn't have the key, this guy might not have been the one to lock her in the cage. If he wasn't the perpetrator, why wouldn't the person in charge put him in the cage with her? Ugh. Nothing was adding up. She needed answers now.

After rolling him back over to get him out of the way of any falling metal, she closed her eyes, concentrated, and extended her claws. She couldn't remember the last time she'd had to shoot fire out of her hands.

Greer took aim at the lock and blasted it with flames—or at least that was her intention. The flames shot back through the bars and nearly caught her on fire. Shit. She immediately withdrew her arm. Not one to give up, she decided to point her hand toward the outside and focus on the bar instead.

The sedative must still be in her body, because while the flames licked and flicked over the bar, the metal never seemed to weaken. Crap. She needed a new plan—one that involved the prone man outside of the cage. Because he was a dragon shifter, he might be able to help.

"You awake yet?" she asked.

When he didn't respond, she became a bit testy. It was bad enough she'd lost one of her favorite shoes, but to be caged was the last straw. There was only one thing to do. Try to heal him so he could help. How much worse could it get?

Chapter Nineteen

ANGELIQUE DID NOT want to leave the amazing tree house. Thane's clever ways of sealing up every crevice and crack to make the place lightproof had worked. Either Mange hadn't found them or else he hadn't been able to get in.

"Do you think he didn't know we left town?" she asked Thane. Not that he'd know, but Thane had dealt with criminals his whole life.

"That depends. Do you believe he's only as smart as the person he's inhabited or does he have some innate abilities that he could use?"

She ran her hands through her hair. "He had a lot of abilities when he was in his pure dark light form, but I don't know if when he takes over another person's body, if he will be as smart as they are. I wasn't put into an existing body. Mine was created specifically for me."

"I'm glad it's all you and not leftovers from someone else."

She shivered. "I don't think I could live with myself if someone had to die so I could have a corporeal form."

"Me neither."

"Part of me wants to head back to the realm and tell them that their teaching skills sucked. When they let us loose on another world, they need to provide us with better intel."

Thane chuckled. "You are something else. If as you claim Fate is in charge of you all, do you think Fate should spend his or her day teaching you everything? Where's the fun in that? Fate is probably enjoying seeing how you all do here."

While that was not the sympathetic response she wanted, it did make sense. "I guess, but I hate uncertainty."

"Come on. We should head back. As soon as we exit the forest, I'll see if we can get cell reception. Maybe they found Greer and all is good."

She sagged with relief. "That would be wonderful."

Before they left, they stripped the bed, unsure of when Anderson's parents would need to use the cabin. She didn't see any laundry facilities so she had no idea how they washed or cleaned anything.

The trip back through the forest was hard at times—at least for her. Climbing down the mountain wasn't fun, but eventually they made it. Twice, Thane insisted she hop on his back so he could carry her, which turned out to be the best part of the trip. She loved how strong he was.

Once in the open, he called Griffin who was taking point on the search. "Hey, it's me. Anything?" Thane asked.

She leaned over so she could hear his response. "Nothing yet, but we're still searching. I trust Mange kept his distance?"

"He did."

"Did you think of anything while you were vacationing?" Griffin asked.

"Unfortunately, no. We're headed back to town now."

"See you there."

Thane faced her. "You know, when we were making love, I noticed this delicate pink light shining inside you."

She smiled and dragged a finger down his chest. "When I'm excited, I always glow."

"No, this was different."

She stepped back. "What are you saying?"

"I didn't want to mention it at the time—since I was really enjoying myself and didn't want to be interrupted—but it's possible your ability to shift is growing."

She shook her head. "I can't shift."

"So you've been told. Remember, your realm teachers weren't

always forthcoming. Besides, those in your realm might not know about the power of the Guardians." He puffed out his chest. "We are quite virile." Thane winked.

She chuckled at his antics. Angelique was about to dismiss it until she remembered several strange things had been happening lately. For one, there had been some pressure at the end of her fingertips one time, but she'd dismissed it. She had attributed the heat racing through her body at odd hours to stress. Maybe it had been due to a dragon trying to get her attention. "If I wanted to shift, what would I have to do?"

His eyes slightly widened as if he'd expected her to tell him he was crazy.

"I've never taught anyone, but how about closing your eyes, hold your arms out straight, and focus on becoming a dragon."

She tilted her head to the side. "Really? That's so hokey. There has to be something more to it than that. You don't pose before you shift."

"No, but I've been doing it for over one hundred years. It's second nature. Maybe you should ask Chelsea when we get back. Declan was able to teach her."

"I like that idea." Angelique stepped back, waiting for Thane to shift.

"You aren't even going to try?"

"And fail?" It wasn't in her nature.

Thane drew her to his chest. "I won't think any less of you. Hell, I'll respect you more for trying, even if you don't succeed."

She felt stupid, but for Thane she'd give it a try. "Fine."

Knowing how much space a dragon needed, she stepped back and tried not to have a negative attitude. Things like this were all about belief. She closed her eyes and stretched out her arms.

"Think about becoming a dragon and flap your arms up and down to simulate flying," Thane instructed.

Angelique wasn't sure if she wanted to succeed now. Turning into something almost fifteen feet tall with the ability to fly kind of terrified her. "Here goes."

She pictured the shape of his dragon snout and the long, graceful wings. As if something dark had invaded her, her body started to pull apart. Petrified that Mange had found her, she opened her eyes and wrapped her arms around her body.

Thane rushed over to her and drew her into a hug. "What happened?"

Angelique's breathing came out way too fast. She'd never lost her cool like that before. "I thought Mange was here."

Thane swung her behind him and looked around. "I don't see or sense anyone."

"It's okay. The feeling has passed."

He spun around. "When you felt this darkness, did it feel as if someone was tearing your body apart?"

"Yes. Exactly." She was so thankful he understood.

He framed her face with his palms. "It's supposed to be that way—at least the first time. Your body was trying to change shape."

"Really? Did you see anything happen?" She stretched out her arms and looked for scales.

"No." He wrapped an arm around her waist. "I think that is enough excitement for one day. We can try again later."

Thane was the best. Angelique's nerves were already stretched taut. "I'd like that."

"Ready for your lift home?"

"Totally."

While the view below her of the green landscape, lush forests, and many lakes was spectacular, Angelique couldn't expel the strange feeling of when she'd tried to change into a dragon. If Mange hadn't shown up in Tarradon, she might not have freaked when it felt as if dark light had entered her body. Thane seemed to think it was ordinary, but Angelique would feel more comfortable after speaking with Declan's mate, Chelsea.

The city came into view, and Thane headed to the top of the SinCas building. He landed and then set her down. "Fingers crossed there is some news," she said.

Thane shook his head. "Fingers crossed? Where did you learn that phrase?"

"Chelsea said it once."

He chuckled. "Gotta love Earth. Come on."

Police tape was wrapped around the counter when they entered the jewelry store. Tory was speaking with someone who wore a Custom Cabinets uniform. At least the shattered glass had been cleaned up. Tory squeezed the man's arm and rushed over.

"I'm glad you're here," Tory said. She leaned closer. "Did Mange show up?"

"Thankfully, no," Thane said. "Have you been in contact with Anderson or anyone else?"

"Griffin has done a great job coordinating everything, but there have been no sightings."

"How about Blake Masters' body? Has it been found?" Thane asked.

"No."

Angelique wasn't sure what she thought about that. "Either Mange is learning how to hide his bodies better or worse, he's still in it."

"Shit," Thane said. "We need to know what we're dealing with. Everyone should be on the lookout for this guy. At least we have a name this time."

Angelique grabbed his arm. "No one but us should be anywhere near him. If they spot him, they have to let us know, not attack him."

He smiled down at her. "I know what's at stake, my beautiful white entity."

She hoped he did.

GREER REACHED OUT and placed her hands on the man's shoulder and hips, sending her healing powers through him. Unless he'd hidden the key to the padlock somewhere, he might not be able to get to her even if he awoke.

Concentrating hard to heal him, each pulse that traveled from her to him weakened her body. Crap. The drugs were making her job so much harder. The man groaned, and she released him. Greer needed time to recharge in case he came in after her.

She sat back on her heels. "Hello?" Damn, her voice wobbled. That was so unlike her.

The man grunted once more and then raised a hand to his forehead. He must have opened his eyes because he pushed up on his elbow and looked around. "What the hell?"

"Who are you?" she asked.

The man jerked back around. "What are you doing in a cage? And where are we?"

He seemed to recognize her, but Greer wasn't sure if that was a good thing or not. "That's what I'd like to know."

He sat up and then rubbed his forehead. "You're the woman from the jewelry store."

"Yes, but who are you?"

"Blake Masters. I work at the First Bank of Tarradon."

She must have been transported to another realm because nothing was making sense. "I'm Greer." She saw no reason to advertise she came from the wealthy Caspian family. "What is the last thing you remember?"

He rubbed his stomach and then groaned. "I went to the jewelry store to buy an engagement ring."

She refused to address the disappointment. There was something about Blake that drew her to him. Why though? Hadn't he been the reason she was there? Crap. If she weren't still under the influence of the drug, she might have been able to think more clearly.

"Your mate is human I take it?" Shifters didn't give another shifter an engagement ring. That was reserved for humans.

"Yes."

"What else do you remember?" she asked.

He inhaled and closed his eyes. His hand slipped into his pocket. "I went to pull out a piece of paper with my girlfriend's ring size on it when I felt something sharp."

"It was a syringe. Why did you stab me in the neck?"

He sat up straighter. "Excuse me? I would never do something like that."

Blake Masters sounded sincere, but the fact of the matter was that he had stabbed her.

He doubled over, causing her sympathy to swell. "What's wrong? Are you still injured?" She knew damned well that something bad had happened to him if her reaction to healing him was any indication.

"I don't know." He tugged his shirt out of his pants, and when he lifted it up even Greer gasped. He gently touched the dark brown spot. "Fuck."

"I'm a healer. Take off your shirt. I might be able to help if I can see what's wrong."

Blake shot her a look, but then shrugged. "Can't make it worse, I suppose. Or can you?"

He twisted toward her, acting as if he suspected she had something to do with their situation.

"No. I'm not the bad guy here. If I were, I wouldn't have put myself in a locked cage and thrown away the key."

"I suppose not." Blake ditched his jacket, loosened his tie, and then unbuttoned his shirt.

Once he removed it, when he twisted away from her, Greer's heart broke. His back and arms were completely bruised and tinged with brown. "Do you remember being in a fight?" she asked.

"No why?"

"Your back and arms look worse than your stomach."

He reached around him and winced. "Shit." With effort, he stood and then looked up. "Don't freak, but I'm going to shift into my dragon form to see if I can heal." Blake walked to the far side of the warehouse, out of direct line of sight from the door.

In case their captor returned, Blake would be hidden—at least for a few seconds. "Go for it."

One second he was human, and the next he was a huge sand colored dragon with interspersed black scales. She'd never seen anything like his kind before.

Blake paced for a bit then folded in his wings and stilled. When he closed his eyes, she figured he was working hard to let his dragon do its job.

Greer leaned back against the bars and stretched out her legs, still pissed about losing her shoe. She'd almost dozed when a noise startled her, and something painful invaded her.

In a flash, she sat up. A man with a wolf shifter signature entered the building. He smelled evil. Oh crap. It had to be Mange.

Chapter Twenty

THANE WAS GROWING more agitated by the minute. Angelique wrapped an arm through his and leaned closed. "Since there's not much we can do here, how about coming with me to check out the coffee shop? I want to see how close we are to opening."

Melissa and Shannon had been texting her on and off about the progress. Without a doubt, both deserved a bonus for all the hard work they'd put in to making sure the floors were dry, the place didn't smell of smoke, and the roof was repaired.

Thane looked down at her. "I've been so preoccupied with Greer that I forgot how someone nearly burned down your place. I'm interested to see the progress as well."

Just as they were about to leave, Griffin and Declan walked into the jewelry store. For the next few minutes, they chatted with Thane about the progress of the search for Greer and Mange, aka Blake Masters. It wasn't that Angelique wasn't interested in finding her nemesis, but she figured they'd meet soon enough. She just hoped both she and Thane were together when that happened.

Once his brother and cousin returned to the search, Thane turned to her. "Ready?"

"Yes."

They exited out the side door and turned right toward her coffee shop. Declan had told them that yesterday the Guardians had flown over a ton of buildings, trying to sense shifter signatures, but had come up empty-handed.

She clasped his hand and squeezed. "Don't worry, we'll find her."

"I'm sure we will. The question is when and in what condition?" Thane slowed. "I just thought of something. Do you know if Mange can put a spell on a person to cloak their shifter signature? It would explain why we can't find them."

"I don't know, but in theory I can do it—even if a person is in his human form."

"Really? How long would the spell last?"

"A couple of hours, maybe. A dark entity's abilities might be greater than a white entity's. It would also depend on the curse. I just don't have enough experience in these things to know for sure." She grunted. "Every time I think about it, I become angry and frustrated. Our education sucked."

"Maybe Fate did it on purpose. You're thrown into a deep pool of water, and if you figure out how to swim in time, you live. If you don't—"

"I die. I get it. Still doesn't mean I like it."

Thane rubbed her shoulder. "Remind me never to go to your realm. It sounds terrible."

She hadn't meant to paint it as a horrible place. "Like any realm, it has its good points and its bad."

When they reached the coffee shop, a ton of activity was going on inside. Angelique didn't have her key for the shop with her, but Shannon pushed open the door as soon as she spotted them.

"Welcome back," Shannon said. "I hope you like the changes."

"I'm sure I will."

When Angelique had purchased the shop from another coffee shop owner, she didn't change much. The three of them had talked about what she would do when she had the time and money to decorate to her taste, and now those changes had been made.

Angelique smiled. "You went with the pale green walls. I love it."

"Come see the kitchen. You won't recognize it. Donald has outdone himself."

All three of them headed down the hallway toward the kitchen. "I see we now have cameras back here. Nice."

Shannon smiled. "I thought you'd appreciate that."

Inside the kitchen, Angelique beamed. "Donald, you've performed a miracle."

Her chef blushed. "Always wanted a new stove, but I didn't expect to get it this way."

She looked up. The ceiling had already been fixed and painted. "When do you think the kitchen will be ready to open?"

"The paint will have had time to cure by tomorrow, and I'm almost done with everything in here."

"That's great." The relief surprised her.

"Would you like me to fix you something?" Donald asked.

She turned to Thane. "Would you like a cup of coffee?"

"I would if it comes with pastries."

Donald smiled. "You're in luck. I just baked a batch. I had to make sure the oven was calibrated correctly."

Angelique smiled. "I'm glad you did."

"I'll bring them out with the coffee."

They headed back to the shop and sat by the window. One reason she wanted to come to the shop was to talk to Thane alone. Angelique leaned forward. "We should discuss a few things."

"Like?"

"Like me returning to work once we open."

He shook his head. "It's too dangerous."

Of course, Thane would say that. "If I'm not here, and Mange comes, he might decide to torment me by killing Melissa, Shannon, or Donald."

Thane reached out and cupped her hand. "Once we find him and destroy him, you can be here all by yourself."

"That will happen sooner or later, but when? You can't put your life on the line either. I know stuff is happening in the province that some of the Guardians are trying to solve."

"True. What do you suggest?"

"How about we spend a few hours a day here, and then I spend a few hours a day with you at the mine or wherever you need to be? I don't think we should ever be apart."

He pressed his lips together. "What if I have to fly someplace? It's not like you can come with me. While I can carry you, if a dragon engages me in battle, I might drop you."

She crossed her arms. "Then I'll learn to shift. Somehow."

Donald stepped out of the kitchen and delivered their coffee and pastries. "I have to say it feels damned good to be back up and running."

Angelique smiled. "Thank you for everything."

Once Donald returned to the kitchen, Angelique took a bite of her pastry and moaned at the delicious blend of flavors. She then sipped her steaming coffee. "I hadn't realized how hungry I was."

Thane grinned. "Non-stop sex will build up an appetite like no other."

She laughed, the sensation energizing her. "I'm going to call Chelsea to see if she can give me any pointers about shifting."

"Good idea."

When Declan's mate answered, animals were barking in the background. She must be at the shelter taking care of things until a new owner could be found. Angelique explained what happened when she tried to shift.

"Hmm. I can't say I felt anything dark inside me, but it was quite different than shifting into my wolf form. I did think I would fly apart. The stretching can definitely be scary. I recommend you picture a dragon clearly before attempting to shift. In my case, I have to think whether I want to be in my wolf form or my dragon form."

"That might work." They talked a bit more about a few other techniques. "Thank you."

She disconnected and told Thane what Chelsea said. He took a big bite of the Danish and held up a finger until he finished eating. "You could ask Lily about shifting too. She was a human and had no experience with changing shape."

"I'll give Chelsea's method a try first. If that doesn't work, I'll consult Lily."

He smiled. "No time like the present! We can do a little work behind the mine where it's private. There will be a lot of other people close by, which should prevent Mange from trying anything."

"I'm game."

If Angelique could shift, the two of them would for sure be able to defeat that dark bastard.

"WELL, WELL, GREER. I'm happy to see you're still in your cage and none the worse for wear," the newcomer said. Arms crossed with a vicious sneer lifting his lips, he was wearing dirty jeans, brown sandals, and a gray T-shirt with a plumbing company logo on it.

She'd never seen this man before but from the ugly waves pouring off him, Mange was inside. She didn't dare glance over at Blake for fear of giving away his presence. Blake pressed his back against the wall. Unless this man moved closer to the cage, Blake would remain out of sight.

Hoping to keep the newcomer distracted, she crawled over to the edge of the cage. "Mind telling me why you stabbed me in the neck?"

Granted, the bodies were different, but if Blake was to be believed—along with the horrible wounds on his body—he was a pawn in all of this.

"I want Angelique."

That was what Angelique claimed. "Why? You looking to die?"

He laughed. "I believe the last time she and I ran into each other, it took a team to bring her back to life. I made an error in judgment in not infusing her with enough dark light. I won't let that happen again."

As much as Greer wanted to get out of her cage and claw his eyes out, she understood Mange's incredible power. If he left this man's body, he could enter hers, and then she'd be as good as dead. That begged the question of how had he left Blake's body and not killed him? No doubt he believed he had, or he'd be asking about him.

"I'd be happy to set up a meeting between you and Angelique, though I bet my brother will want to come too."

The man grinned. "The more the merrier. I would like nothing more than to destroy both of those do-gooders."

"What do you have against them?" If she kept him talking, it would give Blake more time to recover. Not that he would succeed against Mange, but perhaps if his beef was with Angelique, the newcomer might just take off.

"Dark entities are born to destroy all white entities."

"Who's to say this white entity won't destroy you first?"

He laughed. "She's weak. It's why she needs to be eliminated."

"I see." Greer kept her gaze solely on the man's face, refusing to react to the fact Blake had unfolded his impressive wings.

"If you lend me your phone, I can ask Angelique to come here, assuming you tell me where I am."

He smiled, but his eyes failed to light up. "We'll be in touch."

Greer tried to stand, but her back rammed against the bars, sending a wave of pain through her weak body. "You can't leave me here. I need water and food." She tried not to beg, but her demand sounded too much like a whine.

"Deal with it." The man stopped and looked around. "Where is the body of the man I was in?"

Shit.

Just then, Blake emerged from the alcove and attacked. Claws extended and fire shooting from his mouth, he dug his talons into the man's shoulder. The shriek that followed was short-lived. The man collapsed to the ground a second later. It might have been Greer's imagination but a dark shadow passed by one of the overhead windows and then was gone.

"Blake, stop. He's not here anymore."

The dragon let go and then shifted back into his human form. Because he hadn't had on his shirt before he'd shifted, he was still bare-chested. Greer was rather impressed with his physique, especially now that the bruises, and what she suspected had been burn marks left behind when Mange had exited his body, were gone or had mostly faded. His dragon had done a good job of healing him.

This view of the healthy man stirred so much inside her that she immediately turned her head. With Mange gone, though certainly not dead, they needed to escape. Lust had no place now, especially when the dark entity could return at any time.

Normally, it would be hard to explain the dead body on the floor to the cops, but with the huge charred mark on his back, Anderson would believe her when she told her cousin that Mange had come and gone.

Blake didn't even look at her. Instead, he walked over to the prone man. "I didn't plan to kill him."

"You didn't. A dark entity did." She felt almost silly saying those words since he wouldn't even know what they meant. Now wasn't the time to discuss it however. "Listen, you need to help me out of the cage. We don't want this guy coming back, possibly with others."

Blake spun toward her. "News flash. This guy isn't going to rise from the dead anytime soon."

Shit. "Can you just shift and pull open the bars. I'll explain everything when we get out of here."

Actually, she was going to let Thane explain it to him. It might be better for Blake's sake to kind of keep him out of the loop. The fewer people who understood what this dark entity was capable of, the better. Knowing Anderson though, he'd have to arrest Blake for drugging her. It didn't matter that he might not have been himself at the time. The only reason she questioned that he could possibly be involved was the fact that Blake was still alive and none of Mange's other victims had survived.

"Sure."

Blake stood back, shifted into his dragon form once more, and then moved toward her. In order for him to grab a hold of the bars, he had to open his wings and drape them over the cage.

She might have been a dragon herself, but she didn't remember being this close to another one quite like this before—other than the few times she'd been in battle. As she caught sight of her yellowish-white scales pulsing under her skin, her heart fluttered. What the hell was wrong with her? Her life was in danger. She shouldn't be thinking about sex. Besides, the man had a fiancée—or would as soon as he bought her a ring.

With a strength that seemed to equal Thane's, Blake tore back the bars wide enough for her to crawl out. As Greer moved through the opening, Blake stepped back and returned to his human form.

"Thank you," she said. Standing caused her to wince. "Ready to get out of here?" She slipped off her remaining shoe, still pissed about losing its mate.

"What about him?" Blake nodded to the half burned body.

"I'll call the police when we get back to town."

"While I believe I did nothing wrong, I have a feeling you're going to tell a different story."

"I'll tell the truth."

Blake held up both hands. "As you believe it to be."

Chapter Twenty-One

EVEN THOUGH IT had been Thane's idea for Angelique to shift, now that she was about to, he wasn't sure this was a good thing. For starters, if she succeeded, his stubborn mate would want to go with him when he fought. Without training, a dragon shifter with any experience could do her irreparable harm.

On the other hand, he didn't want a repeat of what happened when he'd been in the sky, and Angelique had been looking on. If he did battle with a shifter that Mange had inhabited, and the dark entity escaped, Angelique could take to the air. Hopefully, Thane could teach her how to outmaneuver Mange. Thane refused to factor in the concept that no animal was faster than the speed of light.

For the first time in his life, Thane felt helpless.

"I'm ready," Angelique said.

"I'll shift too just in case you need help."

"I'll be fine."

His beautiful mate held out her hands and closed her eyes like she had before. This time, she seemed calmer. Her lips suddenly thinned, and then her hands turned into claws. A second later, she shifted. Thane was about to congratulate her, but he was too stunned by her beauty to even comment. He'd never seen a white dragon shifter. It made sense in a way given Angelique was basically pure light, but maybe it was the delicate pink scales woven among the white that gave her an other-worldly look.

"I did it!" she telepathed.

Before he could respond, Angelique flapped her wings and rose, looking like a Phoenix rising. She was breathtaking.

"How's the view from up there?"

"Incredible."

Angelique turned and headed east. Where was she going? Overachiever. Thane shifted and shot upward. He was beside her in a flash. *"You do know that if anyone sees a white dragon shifter, people will talk."*

"So?"

"You don't think Mange will know who you are and hence where you are?"

Angelique stilled. *"Damn."*

Without any direction from him, she made a big arc and returned to the mine. Her landing wasn't the most graceful, but at least she hadn't crashed. Once on the ground, her dragon didn't move for a moment. Then she began to shift back, and he followed suit.

Once human, Angelique ran over to him. "Thank you for insisting I try. It almost makes me want to go back to my realm and tell them they were wrong about so many things."

He didn't need her to leave and not be able to return. "Sometimes it's better to leave well enough alone." Thane's internal senses sharpened, and he glanced to the sky. "Oh, my goddess, it's Greer!"

His joy was short-lived when he realized another dragon shifter was right behind her. He turned to Angelique. "Get inside the safe house."

"No. If that is Mange, Greer wouldn't be leading him here." She tugged on his arm. "If Mange followed her without her knowledge, we need to be together to defeat him."

"Fine, but stay behind me." Thane stepped in front of her as his cousin and this unknown dragon shifter landed.

When Greer and this other person both shifted into their human form, Thane let his emotions overtake him. When he didn't sense anything evil from this guy, he rushed to Greer and hugged her. "Thank goddess you're okay."

"I'm fine." She held up a red shoe. "You see the other one?"

Happy that her humor had returned, he nodded. "Tory made

sure it wasn't thrown out."

When the man next to her stiffened, Thane faced him and immediately recognized him as Blake Masters, the man who'd stabbed Greer. He stepped between them. "What are you doing here?" *And how are you still alive?*

Angelique rushed up to them. "Thane, that's not Mange."

"I know, but if Mange isn't involved, it means Mr. Masters kidnapped Greer."

Greer grabbed his arm. "No. Mange took over his body and made him do it."

That made no sense. "How? He'd be dead if that were true."

She let out a breath. "Can we go inside and discuss this? I'm really thirsty and hungry."

"Sure." If Angelique didn't indicate this Blake fellow was Mange, he saw no harm in interrogating him.

Greer led the group across the field. While she appeared to be walking okay, her shoulders were slightly stooped, almost as if the drugs had yet to completely wear off. He would have thought her dragon would have dispelled them on the flight back.

She turned to him. "I don't have my key to get in."

There was no way he was taking a potential criminal into the safe house. "We can talk in the office." He glanced over at Blake. Hopefully, his cousin understood the need for caution.

"Fine, but I need to get inside."

She probably wanted to change and eat something. "Sure."

Once he let her in, Thane escorted this man to his office. "I'm going to call Anderson Caspian, a detective with the APP."

"Good," Masters said. "He'll need to take care of a body that Greer claimed somebody by the name of Mange escaped out of—whatever that meant. She said she'd explain when we arrived here."

That almost made sense, but before they told this possible Mange accomplice anything, he wanted Anderson there since he'd be the one dealing with him. After a quick phone call, his cousin said he'd be there pronto.

"Is Greer going to be okay?" Masters asked.

"What's it to you?" Thane couldn't help but be bitter. He'd seen the video of this man stab his cousin in the neck and then carry her down the hallway.

"Greer told me what I did, but I don't remember any of it."

"I guess we need to let the cops decide where to go from here." Thane couldn't stand being near this guy.

Angelique stood. "Can I get you anything to drink?" she asked Blake.

"Yes, ma'am. I'd love a glass of water and anything you can scrounge up to eat. Even though Greer was kept in a cage and I wasn't, there was no food or water at the warehouse. I still can't figure out what that man's game plan was. He told us all he wanted was someone by the name of Angelique."

Shit. Thane spun around. "Tell me everything."

"Thane, cool off. If Greer said it was Mange, then it was Mange. If he wants me, that confirms it."

"How can you remain calm?"

"Trust me, I'm not. I'm going to go get water and look for food."

"Second door down the hallway, take a left. It's our kitchen. We have everything you'll need in there."

"I'll supply us with a feast. I have a feeling this will take a long time."

ONCE ANDERSON ARRIVED, Thane set up the computer feed for Blake to watch. It clearly showed him reaching into his pocket, looking at the syringe, and stabbing Greer.

Blake buried his face in his hands. "I can't believe it."

"Can you explain what happened?" Anderson asked.

Greer had returned, looking as if she'd showered. When she walked in the office, she sat next to Blake, which kind of surprised

Angelique. After all, this man had kidnapped her.

"No. Like I've told you, I remember walking into the jewelry store and then sticking my hand in my pocket for the piece of paper with my girlfriend's ring size. Instead of the paper, I felt something sharp and pulled it out. That's all. It's a blank until I woke up on the floor of a warehouse."

"Let's assume that is true. Just before you entered the store," Anderson said, "do you remember a man passing you? We think he might have slipped the syringe into your pocket."

Blake shook his head. "I was too excited about getting the ring to notice much of anything else."

"Anderson," Greer said. "I believe him. Did he drug me? Yes, but if you'd seen the burn marks on his stomach, back, and arms, you'd know that Mange was inside him for a while before he escaped."

Thane looked over at Angelique. "Have you known anyone who's survived a dark entity taking over his body?"

"Not personally, but like I said before, it's possible. Remember, I weakened him. I'm thinking my light caused enough harm that he had to exit in multiple places, allowing Blake to live."

Anderson's phone rang. "Excuse me," he said as he pushed back his chair and stood.

Most likely because everyone in the room had perfect hearing, Anderson stepped outside of the room. When he returned, he sat down. "We found the man at the warehouse who was wearing a plumber's shirt. His name was Rich Cromwell. The burn marks on his body are consistent with the ones created by this dark entity."

"If this dark entity was powerful enough to kill this plumber, why did I live?" Blake asked.

Anderson glanced over at Angelique. "Any theories?" he asked.

Angelique turned to Blake. "You might have been stronger than the others."

"It's possible. So now what?" Blake asked.

Anderson shoved back his chair again. "I'm afraid I'll have to take you in." He held up a hand. "I believe that you might have been taken over, so to speak, by this dark entity, but we can't just take your word for it."

"What's it going to take to prove my innocence?"

"We'll need Mange to confess."

Blake dragged a hand down his jaw. "If he's as powerful as you say, I don't see that happening."

"Maybe not."

Anderson escorted Blake out, and Angelique was pleased he didn't try to flee. The whole time Greer said nothing. Clearly, she was trying to clarify her own thoughts.

"What do you think, Greer?" Angelique asked.

"I'm still a bit confused, but I'm more afraid for you. If you saw that man's face—the one that Mange was in—he means to kill you."

"Just because he wants to, doesn't me he's going to. Look, as I see it, Fate wouldn't have given me the incredibly important role of watching over all of the Guardian children only to allow one of our own to kill me." She looked over at Thane and clasped his hand. "I think Fate put Mange in our path to bring us closer."

He rubbed his thumb over the back of her hand. "I hope you're right."

THE NEXT FEW days were terribly tense for Angelique. True to Thane's word, he went with her to the coffee shop every morning, since it was her busiest time. She wanted to be there to let everyone know that it was business as usual.

So many of the town's people came out to support her that she had to hire another server. That worked out well for her since it allowed her to spend quite a lot of time with Thane at his office. He'd closed his training facility until Mange was dead.

As an added bonus, when he trained some of the other Guardians behind the mines, he included her in the exercises. Some of the dragon maneuvers were definitely too difficult for her to master, but she was learning a lot. When she wasn't in the air, Thane had her master the exercise course, which she grew to enjoy.

As for flying? The thrill she expected never came. Maybe it was because her only mode of transportation for eons had been teleporting from one place to another. Having to work to stay aloft wasn't that big of a thrill. Only when Thane had carried her, had it been exciting, as she could be pressed up against his chest.

After three long days of working out, Angelique decided to leave the battling to those who loved it—like Nessa, Tory, and most of the men. Declan was a natural in the sky, but next to Thane and him, she'd have to say Griffin was the biggest surprise. His ability to stay calm while under attack was impressive. It would serve him well when the time came to fight.

Chapter Twenty-Two

"**H**OW ABOUT WE hit the showers and then indulge in a pastry at your shop?" Thane asked after a particularly long training session.

He was so sweet. He understood how much she enjoyed being among friends. "That sounds great, but I promised you that we would stay at your job for the afternoon."

Thane smiled. "Sometimes even I want a break."

"Aw, you're human after all." Angelique punched him in the arm and then stepped back.

"Funny girl. Let's go."

They were still staying at the safe house, which would have to change soon. Angelique was beginning to feel hemmed in. She wanted a place where she and Thane could run around naked if they wanted.

After cleaning up, they both took to the skies. Thane said she could never get too much practice. He also claimed it was safer to fly than to drive—at least until Mange was dead. Considering all that had happened, Angelique was happy to do as Thane suggested.

They landed in the alley behind her coffee shop, because it afforded her plenty of room in case she misjudged the space. Once down, they both shifted. Smells from the kitchen wafted toward them. Instead of going through the rear entrance the customers used, she entered through the kitchen.

"Hey there," Donald said. "This is a nice surprise. Twice in one day."

Angelique smiled. "It is for us too."

Not wanting to hold up her cook, she and Thane entered the hallway and then turned right toward the coffee shop. For late afternoon, the place was quite full, and she couldn't be prouder of how far she'd come.

Thane looked down at her. "Looks like business is really picking up."

"Yes." Angelique had worked hard to achieve this level of success.

Shannon was at the counter and waved. Angelique led Thane over to one of the few remaining booths that overlooked the street entrance and sat down.

Shannon rushed over. "I didn't expect to see you again today."

"Thane put me through my paces on the obstacle course. I need a cold iced tea and a peach cobbler to get me through the rest of the day."

Thane smiled. "Make it two."

"Coming right up."

While they waited, Angelique decided now might be a good time to discuss their living arrangements. "Once all this stuff is over, we'll need to think about where we want to live." She leaned forward. "I'm ready to settle down, Thane."

"I totally agree. You have a nice place, though it is a bit small."

That was the problem. "And your place belongs to you."

He chuckled. "That's usually how it works."

"What do you say we find a place of our own—a home to raise a family in? It'll be fun to search for houses."

He leaned back. "I'm game, but I thought you said being a white entity, you couldn't...you know."

"Have kids? I said that, but I was told I couldn't shift either. I don't want to rule anything out."

"I like your positive attitude. I can guarantee you that I'll like trying." He winked, clearly trying to keep things light.

As Shannon returned with the tray carrying their drinks and pastries, a wave of darkness filled Angelique. What the hell?

Shannon set down the tray. "It's time, Angelique." Her voice sounded funny—much too deep and highly threatening.

Oh shit. "How could you?" Angelique spat out. Mange had taken over Shannon, and the idea of him killing her nearly incapacitated Angelique.

Thane slid out of the booth and grabbed the woman. He must have sensed her darkness too.

Angelique jumped out as well. "Please let Mange go," she whispered to Thane. "I don't want to make a scene and scare my customers." Angelique turned to Shannon. "How about if the two of us discuss this in my office?"

"Not on your life. I want all of your patrons to watch you die. If you do manage to weaken me, I'll just jump into another body." Mange laughed, and the nearby crowd quieted into stunned silence. "Ah, yes, I can see it now. People will be screaming and dashing for the exit after I kill a few of them."

Several of her customers were looking on in horror, while many were already making a beeline for the back entrance. Attempting to kill her was one thing, but threatening innocent people in her coffee shop took it to a whole other level.

Both of Shannon's arms raised, and then Mange blasted Angelique with more darkness than she thought possible. Staggering back, she bumped into the booth and had to grab hold to keep from landing on the floor. Heart pounding and her insides on fire, she used much of her remaining strength to shoot her white light into Shannon. Angelique feared she might harm or even kill her assistant, but she had no choice.

Thane stood back and stared at Mange. A second later, he too leveled his arms. White light poured out of him. Shannon's eyes widened, and then she searched for what was probably an escape plan. Steps faltering, she rushed down the hallway and ducked through the kitchen door.

Angelique's breath and sanity finally returned. "She's in the kitchen. I have to go after her."

"I'll head around back and come in through the kitchen door to cut her off. Together, we'll take Mange down." Angelique loved how Thane, the consummate warrior, had an instant battle plan.

Inhaling to steady herself, Angelique went after her nemesis on rather shaky legs. When she reached the kitchen, Donald was kneeling over Shannon who was sprawled on the floor, her body limp. He looked up at Angelique, grief stricken. "What happened?"

Shannon's eyes had glazed over, but by some miracle, she appeared to be still alive. "Call an ambulance," Angelique commanded. As much as Donald deserved an explanation, there wasn't time.

She didn't sense any evil around either of them, which meant Mange was on the hunt for a new body. Since he didn't return to the main room, he must have escaped under the crack in the kitchen entrance door.

With her energy slowly returning, Angelique ran out the back. Thane was in the alley, looking around.

"Anything?" she asked.

"No."

A blast of evil swooped in. Thane's hands clenched at his sides and his eyes went wide. "I just felt something." He grabbed his chest and took a step back.

"Thane, what's happening?" Angelique feared Mange might have taken over his body.

At the horror of that thought, her throat closed up and her muscles weakened. She feared the worse for him.

"He's inside me, trying to…" Thane telepathed.

"What are you going to do now, Angelique? Kill the man you love?" Mange grinned as the words came from Thane's lips.

"You have to fight him," she begged her mate.

"I'm sending as much white light through him as I can, but he's pounding me with his darkness."

"Hold on."

Damn Fate. Angelique had no idea what sending her light through Thane would do to him. For certain, Mange would send all of his darkness through him to get to her, and that might kill her mate first.

Once more, she had no choice.

Thane stood tall. *"Give it all you got,"* he telepathed. *"Don't worry about me."*

"It might kill you."

Mange powered up again and blasted her, only this time his powers were less than before. Thane's white light was helping to kill the son of a bitch. The question she couldn't answer was whether it would work fast enough to save him?

"Do it, Angelique! Now!"

Concentrating, she raised her hands and shot white light from her fingertips. Thane faltered and grabbed his stomach. It was as if a hundred men were hitting him in the gut. He bit down on his lip and nearly doubled over.

Help me, Fate, she pleaded.

Angelique's vision blurred, and her knees gave way. A second later, she was one with Thane, just like she'd been when Declan was trying to save his mate.

"Thane, I'm here. Shift and take flight."

"Angelique. Is that really you? I can see you on the ground. Your eyes are closed."

Shit. *"I had to leave my body. Now please, Thane. Shift."*

As if she'd been hit by a fifty-foot wave, she tumbled and spun, her white light bouncing everywhere inside him. While she wasn't in her physical body, she was able to experience everything that was happening to Thane—pain mixed with determination.

"How high?" Thane asked, though she could tell it took a huge effort to even stay conscious, let alone fly.

"This is good. Let your dragon heal you while I take out Mange."

An evil laugh rang in her ears. While she didn't hear the dark entity speak, his evilness was edging its way into her. Drawing on all her strength, along with her love for Thane, she expanded her light in every direction.

Just as her attempt faded, a second blast surrounded her, bathing her in warmth and love.

"I'm here," Thane telepathed.

Together, they pummeled their enemy, but Mange gave back as good as he got. She couldn't die now, not when she'd just found Thane. Intense pain rattled her cells, and she seemed to be coming apart at the seams. In agony and barely able to hang on, Angelique expelled all of the light until she was no more.

"ANGELIQUE, WAKE UP!"

It was Thane's voice. She cracked open her eyes. She was now in her body on the ground in the alley behind her store. Sirens sounded in the background, and Thane's magnificent face was leaning over her.

"What happened?" she telepathed, needing to know she was talking to Thane and not Mange.

"He's gone."

Gone? She couldn't wrap her mind around that fact. Angelique pushed up on her elbows and then extended her hand. "Help me up." With care, Thane pulled her to her feet. "The last thing I remember was that we were losing the fight—or so I thought."

"I can't be certain, but when I felt your love and warmth pouring through me, it was so strong and amazing that my dragon gave me a boost of energy. We dumped everything we had inside of us. Technically that might not have been what actually happened, but it felt that way."

"Maybe it did. Then what?"

"I could feel you leave me, and it scared the daylights out of me. I thought I'd lost you." He gathered her in his arms and held her tight. Thane kissed the top of her head, and Angelique's body woke up.

While she wanted to be in his embrace forever, she had to know where Mange was. "And Mange?"

"It was as if something was leaking out of every cell in my body. I shot to the ground to make sure you were okay, and then I saw this dark shadow hovering over you."

"Mange."

"Yes. Without thinking, I used whatever energy I had left and shot it into him. I was so afraid my white light might have hurt you, but I had to put an end to him."

She ran a hand down his arm. "I had wondered the same thing when I aimed my light at Shannon and then again at you. How did Mange respond?" She had to know he'd never hurt anyone again.

Thane nodded to a pile of dark spots on the ground. "That's what is left of him. He's gone, and good riddance."

Just as she stepped over to Mange's remains, a puff of wind scattered him. "I can't believe we destroyed him, and that he can't harm us anymore." Or so she hoped.

Thane wrapped his arms around her. "I've never been so afraid in my life. When I saw you lying there, I wanted to shoot him with a ball of fire. I didn't though for fear of hitting you."

She chuckled. "It doesn't matter now. We're safe."

An ambulance roared down the alley. "Why are they here? Is it for Shannon?" he asked.

"Yes."

The back door opened, and Donald stuck his head out. "Angelique! Are you okay?"

"Yes, I'm fine. How is she?"

He shook his head. "Shannon is still alive, but that's all. She has a bad burn on her body. I put some ice on it, hoping it would help."

"That's great, Donald. Thank you."

Two paramedics piled out of the truck, and Angelique motioned for them to go inside. They didn't need her interfering, so she remained outside with Thane. "I want to go to the hospital with her. Maybe my white light can help her."

"No. You are not strong enough yet."

"It's all my fault this happened in the first place."

He cupped her face. "You're always going to be stubborn, aren't you?"

She huffed a laugh. "I am when it's in the best interest of someone I care deeply for."

Thane held up a hand. "Fine. I'll fly you to the hospital. We'll get there before Shannon arrives."

"Did I tell you that I love you?" She'd certainly hinted at it but had never actually said those words. They had been too scary to say out loud—but no longer. She wanted to profess her love every single day for the rest of her life.

"No, but I knew. Just like I'm sure you know how much I love you."

"Yes. Your actions told me you did. Now, did someone mention a ride?"

Chapter Twenty-Three

THE NEXT FEW days were touch and go for Shannon, but the doctors never gave up hope. Angelique had snuck in a few times and performed a few spells, which sped up her recovery. The hard part was explaining to Shannon exactly what had happened.

Anderson had interviewed her too, to find out what she remembered, but it wasn't much, thank goodness. Shannon claimed one minute she was delivering coffee and pastry to Angelique and Thane, and the next, she was in the hospital with burns on her stomach, along with a wicked headache.

Shannon reached out her hand and clasped Angelique's. "I'm sorry this maniac was out to get you," she said.

"Well, he can't hurt anyone anymore."

"Thank goodness." Shannon released Angelique's hand and pushed up on her elbows to sit up. "When Melissa stopped by, she said something about the same thing had happened to Greer."

Already the rumor mills had it wrong. "Not to her, but to one of her customers at the jewelry store. Like you, he pulled through."

"I'm so glad. Melissa also told me there were others this dark entity had taken over, but that all of them had died."

"That's true too."

"Then why did I live?"

Shannon deserved to know. Survivors' guilt could be hard to deal with. "I hit you—or rather him—with my white light to weaken him. When he left your body, he didn't have the strength to leave from one spot. It's why your injuries, while severe, didn't kill you."

"Thank you. I know you thought I was asleep when you came

into my hospital room, but I could feel your healing light enter me. It was peaceful and very comforting."

"I'm happy I could help. Did the doctor say when you could go home?" Angelique asked.

"Tomorrow, if I'm lucky."

A nurse entered the room and Angelique stood. "Take a few days off and rest. I'll see you when you return."

"Thank you."

Thane was waiting for her in the lobby. "How is she?"

"She'll be fine. Naturally, she's still confused, but that's to be expected."

"Hell, I'm confused, and I was there," he said.

She too had a ton of questions, but they could only be answered by someone from her realm, and she had no intention of going back there to ask—ever. "Speaking of confused, what's the status of Blake Masters and his incarceration? He wasn't responsible for his actions."

"Greer went down to the station yesterday and said she wasn't pressing charges. In light of what happened to Shannon, Anderson let him go."

"I'm glad. If someone other than Anderson had handled the case, I'm not sure Blake would have been released."

"I bet you're right."

They headed out of the hospital and were greeted by the late morning sun. Her skin warmed, and the sweet scent of some blooming flower elevated her mood. She inhaled, loving the freedom of life without Mange. "If Fate ever approached me about what happened, I'd give her—or him—a piece of my mind," Angelique said.

"Why's that?"

"How can you ask that? All this shit with Mange has harmed too many innocent people. Fate has control at all times—or so I've been led to believe. Mange could have been stopped."

Thane wrapped an arm around her waist. "I like to think Mange was let out of your realm in order to bring us together."

"I know I said that too, but then I dismissed it. However, if that was the case, I might consider thanking Fate."

"I've been thinking," he said with a sudden burst of cheer.

"Always a dangerous thing."

He laughed. "Watch it. With all the stuff that has happened, what do you say to a small vacation?"

"While we just had one—albeit one that was short—I'm always up for another one. The problem is that Shannon won't be returning for a couple of days."

"I bet I could ask my Mom to help out."

Angelique smiled. "I bet she'd enjoy that. Where do you have in mind?"

"Hearndon Province. My father has an old friend there by the name of Gregory Kearn who has done very well for himself. So well in fact that he lives in a castle, owns several boats, and has a couple of vacation homes, to name a few things."

"That sounds too good to be true."

"What's better is that Gregory happens to own a private island."

"Ooh. I'm liking the private part."

Thane smiled. "I thought you would. How about we grab some lunch, pack, and fly on over there. It's a long flight across Tarradon, so I hope you are up for it."

"Sure, but how does that work? Do we carry our duffels in our claws?"

He shook his head. "No. Whatever you have in your arms right before you shift will be there when you return to your human form. For example, I have my cell phone in my pocket. If I shift and then return to become human, it's still there."

"Got it. Hey, I heard someone has a birthday in two days."

He waved a hand. "Someone has a big mouth, but just so you know, we only celebrate every ten years since we live so long. I'll be one-hundred and twenty-eight, so no celebration for two more years."

"One-hundred and twenty-eight. Is that all? You are such a

youngster." She was thousands of years old, though now that she'd entered her human body and mated, she'd only live as long as Thane. "Can't you make an exception? I already planned to give you something."

His eyes turned teal. "Oh, yeah. What is it?"

She laughed. "I thought birthday presents were supposed to be a surprise."

Thane held up his hands. "By all means. Keep it a secret. I love surprises."

Now that they were headed to someplace remote, she'd have to tell him something about the gift. "Do you think when we near this island, we can stop at a food store? We'll need to eat if we'll be there for any time. Just be warned; I anticipate using a lot of energy."

When she pressed her body against his, he clasped her shoulders and chuckled. "Though I love having your luscious body pressed up against mine, I don't think the hospital parking lot is the right place to make out."

"You're no fun. I keep forgetting about the prim and proper people on Tarradon." Angelique was only kidding. She was definitely not an exhibitionist.

"Okay, my wild woman. Before I rip off those clothes in plain view of everyone, let's head back to your house. Then we can stop by my place to gather my gear."

"Deal." They both shifted and took off. While flying definitely took more energy than teleporting, there was something nice about the wind in her face. Not only that, but the views in Tarradon were a lot better than in her realm of just plain light.

THE FLIGHT FROM Edendale to Hearndon Province took almost two hours, but the mountain peaks, some of which were snowcapped, took her breath away. Their first stop was to Gregory Kearn's castle, which was amazing. Sure, they'd flown over many stone edifices that had been castles in their day, but none compared to the Kearn castle.

They landed on the front lawn of the estate and shifted. "I've never seen anything like this before." The trees lining the driveway were trimmed without a stray leaf in view, and the flowers underneath were manicured to perfection.

Thane chuckled. "No castles in your realm I guess?"

"Hardly. We had no buildings of any kind. Light doesn't need a bed or food."

"I can't imagine living like that. To come here had to have been such a shock."

"It was, but when I arrived in Tarradon, I occupied myself with spending many hours studying human behavior."

"Such as?"

"Such as what did they like to eat and do, and how did they live? It was overwhelming but exciting at the same time. I will say, during all my studies, I didn't come across anything this grand."

"Come on. I'm sure you'll enjoy Gregory just as much. We can't spend too much time here though. I want to reach the island house before it's dark."

A man in a maroon uniform escorted them inside. Angelique was stunned by its opulence. The paintings lining the long hallway were masterpieces. "I could spend hours looking at these. I especially like this one." Angelique pointed to one of a lily pond. Off to the side, there was the face of a green dragon that looked lost, staring into the water.

Thane placed a hand on her back. "I see I need to show you more of our wonderful world. To round out your education, maybe we'll take a trip to Earth. There are tall buildings there that would blow your mind. Not to mention their Grand Canyon and few other wonders of the world."

She grinned. "Sounds fantastic."

They followed the man to the end of the hallway. He knocked, opened the door, and motioned them in.

Gregory Kearn stood and walked around his desk. He was a

good-looking man with graying hair and a fit body. He smiled and shook their hands.

"It was so nice to hear from you, Thane. How's your father?"

They both sat down. Thane spent the next few minutes talking about his family, as well as the devastation caused by Mange.

Gregory looked over at her. "You were really pure light in a different realm until coming here?"

"Yes." She explained her mission. "I'm still trying to figure out how Mange escaped. If someone did release him, I'd like to know why."

"Apparently, it's in the past now," Gregory said.

"Indeed."

Thane looked over at her. "It's why I wanted her to have a little vacation. You always said we were welcome to visit your private island."

"I did, and I'm thrilled it will be used. When my mate was alive, it was our favorite place to go." He handed Thane some keys that were all labeled, along with a map. "You could fly to the island, of course, but the speed boat might give you a different kind of thrill."

"Thank you, sir." Thane stood and Angelique followed.

"Can you direct us to a grocery store?" she asked. "It's Thane's birthday in two days, and I want to bake him a cake." Along with a big dinner.

"Of course."

"A cake? The brownies were a disaster," he telepathed.

"Just you wait." She might have been offended, but she knew how much he enjoyed their chocolate licking fest. After they'd mated, they had cooked the brownies, but they came out too hard to consume.

After they said their goodbyes, they headed to the grocery store where she asked Thane to pick up food for the next few days while she purchased the ingredients she'd need to celebrate his birthday. Somehow, she managed to pay and leave the store without Thane having any idea what she planned.

They shifted and flew to the marina where at least fifty boats were docked. The lake was so large she couldn't even see land on the other side. "This is awesome," she said.

"Let's hope you feel the same way after the boat trip."

"Do you know how to drive a boat?"

"No, but how hard can it be?" If he hadn't winked, she might have told him she'd fly to this island and wait for him there.

After locating the Beth Ann, the speedboat named after Gregory Kearn's deceased mate, they hopped in and stowed their gear under the seat in back.

"Ready?" Thane asked, sounding like a kid.

"Be careful."

He powered up the engine and laughed. "Not on your life."

While his exit out of the marina was careful and calm, once Thane was in open waters, it was like he was flying for the first time.

"Isn't this fantastic?" he called back to her.

Angelique was sitting in the back trying to hold on. She did love the warm salt spray careening off the choppy lake water, but she wasn't sure her back would appreciate all the jarring. Thane had pointed to where they were going, and that the trip wouldn't take more than twenty minutes by boat. She readily admitted this was a ride she'd never forget.

By the time they arrived at the island, Angelique was actually disappointed the joy ride was over. They had to drive around to the back side of the island to dock. When she stepped onto land and looked up, the view of the house on top of the hill was spectacular. "Wow. I kind of expected a small cabin," Angelique said.

"You saw Gregory's main home. He doesn't do anything on a small scale."

"Apparently not."

After Thane tied off the boat, they picked up their food and duffel bags, shifted, and flew up to the cabin. While the front lawn was sloped, Angelique managed to land without incident. She called that progress. Angelique shifted, and when she turned around to face the water, her heart sang. "This is so beautiful."

Thane shifted and stepped next to her. "It sure is. Let's set our stuff down and do a little exploring."

She wondered if his definition of exploring meant they'd be outside or in the bedroom. Since she had been recovering from the battle with Mange—both mentally as well as physically—their lovemaking had taken a back seat. This romantic setting was about to change all that.

The cabin had high wood-clad ceilings and a wooden floor. The sofa was a huge lounge chair built for four that faced the water below. Leaving here in a few days would definitely be hard.

"Let's put the groceries away and then we can check out the view," Thane said.

Angelique's body was already throwing off a ton of light in anticipation of making love with him. For the first time since they first made love, she didn't have to worry about Mange sneaking up on them. It would just be the two of them, and she couldn't wait.

Once they put away the food, Thane poured each of them some wine and handed her a glass. Because a candle sat on each of the side tables next to the lounge chair sofa, he lit both of them. The sun was beginning to set, and the lake had ripples of purples and gold reflecting off of it. "Join me," he said as he motioned she take a seat.

Angelique sighed and dropped down next to him. She stretched out her legs and admired the view. "This is spectacular."

Thane raised his glass. "To us!"

She tapped her glass to his. "To us."

Thane stared at the scenery before turning back to her. "I had no idea how much my life was lacking until I met you."

Embarrassed by his compliment, she deflected it. "You mean your fighting skills were honed after learning to fight something that didn't even have a body?"

"No, silly. I'm serious. Angelique, I'm not an eloquent man, as you well know. Hell, I'm much better showing you, but I need you to believe me when I tell you how much I love you."

Her heart melted. "I love you too, so I guess that settles it."

"What does?"

"If I could figure out how, I'd send a card to Fate and thank her—or him—for leading me to the perfect man."

"I thought you were mad at Fate."

She set down her glass and then dragged a hand down his chest. "Not anymore."

He placed his drink behind him. "Perhaps we should show Fate just how happy we are with her choice."

"Now you're talking."

Thane twisted her to the side and placed her on her back. He then propped up her head with one of the pillows, making her feel like a princess in a castle.

"I hope you're ready to be ravished and loved," Thane said.

Angelique raised her arms, still in awe of the hint of pink under her skin that was flashing and heating up as her desire grew. Thane's whole body was also changing before her eyes. His scales glowed a beautiful gold, and his light brown eyes were filling with swirls of teal, mixed with gold and dark blue. He was everything she could want in a man. "Bring it on."

Chapter Twenty-Four

THANE WASN'T SURE where to begin. He wanted to touch her, hold her, and kiss her all at the same time, but first he needed Angelique naked.

"I can't wait to taste you," he said as he slipped off her shoes and then unhooked her pants.

"Fair warning: what you do to me I intend to do back to you."

"We'll see about that." Before Angelique could help him out of his clothes, he unzipped her pants, pulled both them and her panties down to her ankles, and tossed them on the floor. The sight of her pussy had his cock so hard, he had to adjust himself. "You are so beautiful."

She laughed. "You could at least look at my face when you say that."

He glanced up and winked. "I am looking at you."

Before she could give him more sass, he straddled her and slipped two fingers inside her. Angelique's eyes closed and she moaned, twisting and turning as he searched for the perfect spot. When she gasped, he grinned as he continued to elicit more moans and groans, loving how sensitive she was.

Angelique reached out and grabbed his arms. She then slid her hands up to his shoulders and tugged, pulling him forward. The invitation to kiss her was too strong to deny. When their lips met, his body caught fire with every fiber of his being. He needed her. Now.

He removed his fingers from her pussy and threaded his fingers through her thick blonde hair, working to keep his talons from poking through his skin. When she slipped her hands under his shirt and up his back, she stilled, no doubt finding some of his scales had formed. It couldn't be helped. Angelique was too divine.

Needing to bring her nipples to life, he slid his hands under her shirt and slipped it over her head. If he had his way, she'd be banned from wearing a bra—at least when she was in the house.

A quick flick at the clasp released the offending piece of clothing. As slowly as he could, Thane lowered the straps until her perky breasts revealed themselves.

"This is what I want," Thane said.

Angelique let go of him and covered her breasts. "Fair is fair. Strip."

Thane laughed, loving her sense of humor. "My pleasure."

He eased off the chaise and ditched his clothes in no time. Returning to the sofa, he knelt and grabbed his dick, pumping it up and down a few times in the hopes of enticing her.

"You're mean," she shot back. "And selfish."

Oh, how he loved this woman. "What are you going to do about it?"

"Lick it until it's so swollen, you're in pain from wanting more."

He raised his brows. "Then I'll lick you until you come multiple times."

She crossed her arms. "Actions speak louder than words."

With that sassy remark, she sat up and brushed his hands away. A second later, she was on her knees, bent over, devouring his dick.

Not only was Thane physically at the highest point on this private island, he was soaring higher with each lick. He lifted her hair out of the way and then clutched it tight. He could almost feel her white light enter his body. Seeing her delicate scales pulse under her nearly translucent skin took him to new heights.

Angelique lifted off his cock, cupped his balls, and rose up to meet his lips. Her free hand wrapped around his neck as she kissed him, first with tiny nips and then with more intensity.

She let go and dropped down on her back. Angelique was a vision. Thane pressed two fingers into her opening, thrilled when he hit her most sensitive spot on the first try.

Angelique moaned and panted. "Please, Thane."

Hearing her words of desperation made his teeth sharpen and his need for her grow stronger by the second. He massaged and kneaded her breasts. When her nipples hardened under his palms, he pinched them, which caused her whole body to glow and pulse.

His woman of the light had made him whole, and for that he'd love her forever. Needing her more than ever, Thane guided his dick straight into her wetness. The first thrust had his desire soaring. His intention was to take his time, but when Angelique lifted her hips, his dragon seemed to take over. Together they flew high. Thane leaned forward and pressed his cheek against her shoulder, his gold scales shining brightly.

When his climax threatened to release, he sank his teeth into her neck, and a huge surge of lust, love, and hope converged. Angelique stiffened just as his cock detonated. Her inner walls held him in tight as she yelled out his name.

He swore his vision blurred for a moment, and it was only after his dick stopped throbbing that he was even able to move. Angelique collapsed on the sofa. Minutes later, he withdrew and found something to clean them up with.

Thane stretched out next to her and pulled her to his chest. "We needed this," he said.

Angelique looked up at him. "Yes, and to think we have our whole lives ahead of us."

"We do. Let's hope Fate does its job of keeping those damn gates closed."

Angelique laughed. "We'll see."

When her stomach grumbled, guilt made him sit up. "I guess this means we need to round up some food."

Angelique sat up. "You can watch, but you can't help. I'm making you a birthday dinner. I know it's a day early, but I figure time doesn't really matter."

"You're cooking?"

"Yes." She told him how she'd contacted his mom who taught her how to make his favorite meat pie.

He leaned over and kissed her. "This will be the best birthday present ever."

"Wait until you taste it before you say that."

"I'M QUITE PROUD of this meat pie. I admit the vegetables were a bit soggy, but the salt and pepper did wonders for it," Angelique said.

"I thought it was better than what my mom had ever made."

"You are such a sweet man." Angelique sighed. "Even though I'm full from the meal, I want to try the cake. The box claims that all I need to do is add eggs and water and the cake almost bakes itself."

"Sounds simple enough," Thane said.

Angelique let him help her gather what they needed. Together, they dumped the ingredients into the bowl. While Thane mixed it, she prepared the pans to bake it in.

While not all of the batter made into the pans, it was enough to create an excellent looking dessert. While it baked, they talked about where in town they wanted to live.

When the timer chimed, she pulled the cake out of the oven. Thane came over and sniffed. "That looks good and smells good too."

"Happy birthday," she said. "I should have purchased candles. I read somewhere that is the tradition."

He smiled. "A highly overrated one. Let's taste it."

"I need to frost it first."

Thane stepped over to her. "Okay, but it doesn't matter if the cake takes like sawdust. If you made it, I'll love it."

She grinned and held up the spoon coated with the frosting from a can. Thane leaned over and took a bite. "Hmm. Not bad. You might give Donald a run for his money."

"I doubt that."

After the cake cooled a bit, they frosted it. "How about I grab us some wine, and we can sit outside and enjoy our feast?" he suggested.

"I'd love that."

With their two slabs of dessert that almost looked edible, Thane and she headed outside. He pulled the two chairs next to each other and then set the glasses of wine on the side tables. "Let me get the candles from inside."

He returned with them and placed them in the glass containers designed to keep out the wind. He sat down and held up his glass. "To my mate, the woman who fills me with light and love with every look."

She tapped her glass to his. "To my hero, my mate, and the reason I even exist. Happy birthday."

They sipped their wine. "You told me you don't have a birthday, because you've always existed."

"That's true."

"Want to share mine?" he asked.

She grinned. "I can't think of a better day to have one."

Ah, yes, life with Angelique would be challenging and fun. She provided so much love, he hoped his heart didn't burst from all the joy.

I hope you enjoyed reading Angelique and Thane's story as much as I enjoyed writing it.

Don't forget to sign up for my newsletter *to receive three free books, as well as up-to-date information on my stories. If you prefer to only receive notices regarding my releases, follow me on BookBub.*

http://smarturl.it/VellaDayNL

bookbub.com/authors/vella-day

HIDDEN REALMS OF SILVER LAKE (Paranormal)

Awakened By Flames (book 1)

Seduced By Flames (book 2)

Kissed By Flames (book 3)

Destiny In Flames (book 4)

Passionate Flames (book 5)

WERES & WITCHES OF SILVER LAKE

A Magical Shift (book 1) – FREE

Catching Her Bear (book 2)

Surge of Magic (book 3)

The Bear's Forbidden Wolf (book 4)

Her Reluctant Bear (book 5)

Freeing His Tiger (book 6)

Protecting His Wolf (book 7)

Waking His Bear (book 8)

Melting Her Wolf's Heart (book 9)

Her Wolf's Guarded Heart (book 10)

His Rogue Bear (book 11)

PACK WARS (Paranormal)

Training Their Mate (book 1) – FREE

Claiming Their Mate (book 2)

Rescuing Their Virgin Mate (book 3)

Loving Their Vixen Mate (book 4)

Fighting For Their Mate (book 5)

Enticing Their Mate (book 6)

Boxed Set (books 1-3)

Boxed Set (books 1-4)

Complete Box Set (books 1–6)

Author Bio

Want 3 FREE books? Sign up for my newsletter.

COPY AND PASTE INTO YOUR BROWSER:
smarturl.it/o4cz93?IQid=MLite

Check out my latest interview on You Tube:
youtube.com/watch?v=sQo5pyyVMDI

Not only do I love to read, write, and dream, I'm an extrovert. I enjoy being around people and am always trying to understand what makes them tick. Not only must my books have a happily ever after, I need characters I can relate to. My men are wonderful, dynamic, smart, strong, and the best lovers in the world (of course).

I believe I am the luckiest woman. I do what I love and I have a wonderful, supportive husband, who happens to be hot!

Fun facts about me

(1) I'm a math nerd who loves spreadsheets. Give me numbers and I'll find a pattern.
(2) I love photography, so I'll be posting pictures—especially of my Costa Rican adventure.
(3) I also like to exercise. Yes, I know I'm odd. Not only do I lift weights, I love to hike and walk on the beach (yes, it sounds like an ad for a date).

I love hearing from readers either on FB or via email (hint, hint).

Social Media Sites

Website:
www.velladay.com

FB:
facebook.com/vella.day.90

Twitter:
@velladay4

Gmail:
velladayauthor@gmail.com

Google:
plus.google.com/u/0/116041077486216602121/posts

Instagram:
@dayvella

www.ingramcontent.com/pod-product-compliance
Lightning Source LLC
Chambersburg PA
CBHW020953180626
46814CB00003B/1067